It's not you

BECCA SEYMOUR

RAINBOW TREE PUBLISHING

For information, contact the author:
authorbeccaseymour@gmail.com

Editing: Hot Tree Editing

Cover Designer: BookSmith Design

Publisher: Rainbow Tree Publishing

E-book ISBN: 978-1-922359-44-5

Paperback: 978-1-922359-45-2

Hayley.
I'm so pleased we found our way back to each other.
Love you.

Sore in the best of ways and smiling far too widely for this time in the morning, I stretched, pulling my arms from under the covers. With the angles of the light streaming through the windows, I knew it was maybe seven, if that.

But I had no regrets about how early it was.

Even though I'd stumbled into bed super late last night, my mouth on his, our arms wrapped around each other, which meant that I'd probably only had four hours sleep, my tired eyes were worth it.

There was no question last night *was* worth it. And considering the way Billy and I connected, the happy bubble in my gut told me I was pretty sure *he* was worth it too. I'd dropped my guard enough to warm up to the idea of building a relationship that could quite possibly be something extraordinary.

It sounded completely over the top, but we'd been dancing around each other for months, developing our friendship, sharing meals and conversation. And last night everything had changed.

I smiled again and turned my head to the side, for the first time becoming aware of the quiet. I was alone in Billy's bed. I reached out and felt the cold sheets where he'd lain last night with me wrapped around him. Sitting up, I listened carefully, hoping for telltale signs of the coffeemaker or breakfast being made.

When only the ticking clock on the wall reached my ears, a ball of dread formed, growing with my unease. Hauling my ass out of bed, I searched for my shorts, spotting them at the end of the bed with my tee. They hadn't been there last night.

I dressed quickly, my anxiety spiking at the stillness of the house. Despite trying to not overthink and simply assume the worst, I took a few fortifying breaths before reaching for the bedroom door handle, pulling it open, and leaving the room.

With every step I took through the empty hallway, then the empty kitchen, leading to the empty open living space, the pounding in my ears accompanied me. "Billy." My voice sounded loud in the quiet, making me wince.

A sound from toward the back of the house caught my attention. I exhaled in relief and headed back to the kitchen, my gaze immediately landing on Billy entering through the book door.

"Hey," I said, my smile back but nowhere near as bright as when I first woke.

He paused before he fully entered the kitchen, his head jerking upward, his gaze landing on mine. My next words fled when I saw the look in his eyes, the misery evident on every inch of his face.

Straightening up, I tensed, knowing this look, and even without his words, I latched on to the steel needed to protect myself, arm myself for whatever he would say.

"Lawrence." The hardness of my name sounded strange compared to the soft gasps and groans I'd heard him say it with but a few short hours ago. "I…." Billy worked his jaw, before it fixed in a determined grimace. "I have things to do today. I was just coming to get changed."

"Okay…," I said slowly, trailing off and hoping he'd see that as an invite for an explanation or an invite. Even though the latter would have knocked me off my feet in surprise.

His eyes connected with mine. The warmth of last night was long gone. "I shouldn't have let last night happen. I'd had too much to drink, and it was wrong of me to take advantage of you like that."

As he spoke, my brows dipped. Take advantage? Since I'd been cold sober, wasn't I the one who would have technically taken advantage since he'd been the one drinking?

I opened my mouth to speak, but didn't have the chance as he continued, "It was a mistake. I'm sorry. It won't happen again. The last thing I want is to make this awkward or difficult for you, so I'll be sure to stay out of your way."

There was no opportunity to respond, to question or challenge or even call bullshit. He strode past me, this time his gaze resolutely not on me, and left me alone in his kitchen.

The ball previously growing in my gut maxed out, forming uncomfortably and weighing heavy. I swallowed my hurt and confusion, willing the steel to form quicker, desperate for it to be fully erected so I could walk away and not look back.

Putting one foot in front of the other, I kept my eyes on the exit, focused on slowing my breathing.

This would not break me. I clasped the door

handle, ignoring the memory of his sweet words and gentle caresses.

This would not define me. I quietly pulled the door closed behind me, belatedly realizing I was barefoot but no way was I heading back inside. As I stepped into the morning sunshine, I tried to erase the hours of time we'd spent together over the past few months getting to know one another.

And this most definitely would not be the reason I was run out of town again.

Resolved, I didn't look back as I headed toward the one-bedroom apartment I rented from Billy, situated above his garage. Last night had been a mistake all right. And there wasn't a chance I'd allow that to happen again.

CHAPTER ONE

BILLY

I PEERED OUTSIDE MY WINDOW LIKE A STALKER, knowing I needed to drag my gaze away. My desire to catch a glimpse of him was becoming increasingly pathetic. A few months back, there would have been no way I would have admitted that to myself—the whole desperation for a quick glance at the guy thing. But I was long past that. The worst thing was I'd burned that bridge. Set the damn thing on fire. Thrown a few hand grenades on it for good measure.

I'd been an absolute dick, and I didn't think it was possible to *un*dick myself, which sounded way off, but seriously, my behavior had been off-the-charts shit-tastic. And truth be told, I wouldn't have given me a second chance if I were him either.

Lawrence… well, he had been unexpected and too

damn attractive for his own good. Though to be clear, that in no way put the blame on him.

This was all me.

It would have been helpful if he were a dickhead or something, but of course not. He was kind, and funny, and had this shy streak to him that was surprisingly sexy. Not only that, but he also had an ass that I couldn't get off my mind.

One slipup… one night when I should have been too drunk to get anything up, had been epic for the best of reasons but had resulted in nothing but blue balls ever since, and an awkwardness between the two of us that was getting worse rather than better.

And I was 100 percent responsible, completely to blame for my inability to let go. Lawrence had been a distraction I hadn't thought I could afford at the time, but now I knew better.

Finally.

But as time passed by, I figured it was too late to make amends.

The blue door at the top of the external staircase opened, and Lawrence stepped out. His red tee and running shorts left little to my imagination, sparking my memory something fierce. He stretched as he jogged down the wooden steps, reaching the bottom and continuing his routine.

Every damn time he did this, my whole body thrummed with awareness. And I couldn't have looked away if I wanted to. It would have taken a serious distraction to tear me away from the way he flexed and stretched.

I sighed, shaking my head at myself. I was a glutton for punishment, knew as much even as I eyed the way he shifted his arms so his tee rose, lifting the fabric and exposing skin.

And then he looked toward the house, and I quickly edged away, wondering just when I'd turned into this man. Shit, had I still been a cop, I would have arrested myself for this bullshit. I groaned and refocused on what I should have been doing, pulling up the email I'd been hanging around for.

I exhaled before opening it, immediately smiling at the start of the message that was giving me a telling off while letting me know they all loved me and were okay. Attached was also an image of the boys and their latest school pics. They were hilariously dreadful. Teenagers did have a habit of looking awkward. I shook my head, thinking about Clark, knowing he would have gotten a kick out of his eldest looking all gangly with a constipated smile on his face.

As soon as I skimmed the rest of the email, I smiled even wider, this time relieved that I believed her words. I shook my head, amused at the *"sort your shit out and get yourself a man already rather than interfering in my love life!"*

I could practically hear Georgia's disgruntled sigh.

For the past three years, I'd been doing the right thing—or trying to—following my cop-partner's wishes. I indulged in a snort at that, hearing Clark's voice saying, "He wishes he could get a piece of my fine ass," which had been his go-to response often followed by colorful challenges to any idiot who attempted to throw their bigotry in my face—or his.

Clark had been as straight as a ruler, in pretty much all ways. But following the book, being an honest-to-God good cop and the best guy I knew, hadn't stopped our car flipping. It hadn't stopped his head smashing into the window or the car from being crushed, creating shards of steel to be so damn sharp they tore through his femoral artery.

He'd never had a chance.

And me? I'd limped away with a steel rod in my leg, a knee replacement, a few broken bones, and a right eye that would never see well enough to serve again.

I risked another glance outside, surprised to see Lawrence still there, and even more surprised that his gaze was fixed on my house. It was clear he was debating something, and I expected that was whether or not he could handle dealing with me for whatever reason.

Yeah, I was that much of an asshole that the guy didn't want anything to do with me.

I sighed and headed toward the door. Whether he figured out I'd been spying on him or not was neither here nor there. He obviously needed to talk to me about something, and I owed it to the man to make it as painless as possible.

"Hey, Lawrence, need something?" I asked as soon as I opened the door and stepped into the fresh air.

A flush spread across his cheeks, and I doggedly didn't focus on the color, refused to think about how the same pink had spread across his skin when he was mid-orgasm.

"Oh, yeah, hi," he stumbled, making me want to kick myself for being the reason he behaved this way whenever I was around. "Um, the faucet in the bathroom kinda came off in my hand this morning. I think I fixed it," he rushed to say. "But thought you should know just in case." He cast his gaze away, before returning and focusing on anywhere but my eyes.

I sighed internally. "Thanks. You good if I head in and take a look, check it out?"

Lawrence nodded. "That's fine. I'll show you."

It was on the tip of my tongue to remind him I'd be

able to figure it out. The over-the-garage apartment was tiny, but that he wasn't immediately running away from me was something different. I latched on to the opportunity.

As I followed him up the staircase, I willed myself to stop perving on his ass. I allowed one quick peek before focusing over his head. Once inside, he led me to the bathroom and indicated which faucet it was. There was no other option but to brush past him, the space tiny. I did so and controlled my breathing, my reaction. Screwing this up even more by panting over him was not an option.

"So, yeah, I didn't reseal it or anything, but I can head to the store and get something. I wanted to make sure it was right first."

I peered over to where he now stood in the open doorway. This time his gaze connected with mine. Awareness flashed through me, bringing a smile to my lips that he wasn't rushing away. "Thanks. I have some in the house, so no need." I turned back and checked the fittings, crouching down, then shifting to my knees, ignoring the wince when I put pressure on my metal knee.

In this position, I was all too aware I had my ass up in the air. I wondered—hoped, maybe—that I had his attention. Just maybe I could get him interested enough so that I could break down these barriers I'd forced up.

There was nothing more I wanted than to make this right.

I breathed steadily, knowing I was too old to be playing games like this. Forty-three and pining after a guy in his late twenties, and more than that, using my ass in attempt to distract the guy. Christ, I really was a dick.

I flicked a quick glance behind me, rewarded immediately by Lawrence's attention on my ass, his bottom lip clamped between his teeth. Immediately I turned away, thankful as hell that that look from him was enough to prevent my self-loathing from bubbling to the surface.

Finishing up, I double-checked the tightness of the fitting, then eased back. Standing, I turned and said, "You did a great job fixing this up. Thanks."

The smile he offered was tentative, shy, and sweet as hell. "It's all good," he answered with a shrug. "You want to get me the sealant and I'll get it—"

"No, it's cool. I'll do it." The slow trail my gaze made down his body was deliberate as I said, "Aren't you off for a run?" I'd already spotted his skateboard near the front door when I'd entered. And if he wasn't on the death trap of a board, he was off running.

Lawrence shifted a little, the pink in his cheeks returning. The color looked too good there for me to feel guilty for pushing him into a reaction. My bastard status was strong. I knew this, but I needed a reaction from the guy. Only then could I start figuring out the way to make this right.

An apology had already happened.

He'd accepted it graciously, but his hurt had remained palpable. I'd definitely apologize again, but I needed to do more.

"Yeah. Just a short one. Only going to do five miles today."

I nodded, a little envious that five miles were so easy for him. He had youth and fitness on his side. My leg had never quite recovered, my knee especially giving me a problem. At times I felt like a crusty old fart. And with winter doing a number on me, making me ache and limp, I felt that way even more in the colder months.

"I can do this while you're out, if that's okay?" We stepped into the open living space, and I looked around, noticing a few chips of paint and that the place wasn't looking its best.

"Yeah, that's fine."

"Looks like this place could do with a fresh coat of paint too," I added, feeling bad that the place was looking a bit shabby.

"Oh." Lawrence shrugged. "I don't mind. It's dry and comfortable. Plus the air conditioning works," he said, his smile this time fuller and genuine.

"Well, that's good at least, but I do want to get a lick of paint on the walls." I paused, eyes roaming the place, giving my mind time to percolate on the idea that was forming. I internally grimaced at the plan… the playing of games, but spending time with the guy, giving him the chance to see I wasn't always an asshole, was the only possible way forward.

Before I'd ruined everything, our friendship had been growing. We'd shared more than a few beers and meals together. And while I knew he had a birthmark on his right hip, which I'd lavished attention on, I didn't know the deep stuff. I didn't even know if he had family, as he guarded some parts of his past closely. And that was all on me.

I wanted to know the guy.

"So, you working today?"

He shook his head. "No, a rare weekend off. Back in again to open on Monday."

I nodded, aware that a few months ago he'd been given more responsibility at the bar he worked at. "How about when you get back, we can head to the hardware store, and we can pick out some paint?" I followed with a friendly smile, hoping he'd accept, arguably a little desperate he'd take this offer as intended—this was me reaching out.

As he pulled his lips into his mouth and pressed down, his gaze roamed mine. He remained quiet a beat before offering a tentative nod. "Okay. I'll help paint though."

My smile stretched wide. "That'd be great, thanks. Just give me a knock when you're ready."

"Okay." His piercing eyes zeroed in on me, holding contact. "I can do that."

The flip in my gut was immediate. I now needed to make sure I didn't mess this up.

CHAPTER TWO

LAWRENCE

THE MUSIC PLAYING THROUGH MY EARBUDS HELPED ME keep a steady rhythm. The thud of my feet pounding on the pavement offered a comforting beat. I needed the distraction, needed my focus away from Billy and the conversation we'd just had.

Something had shifted. And I wasn't quite sure how I felt about that.

I shrugged the thought away, concentrating on the tune. With my gaze straight ahead, I breathed steadily, pulling in the warm air. Despite the early hour, the temperature was already heating, the norm for August. It was why I got up at the ass crack of dawn to take a run.

What I hadn't expected was for Billy to already be awake.

The routine kept me focused as well as ensuring I stayed fit. For too many years, I'd been at the mercy of being all but trapped by my mother's routine and expectations. It meant that for the past ten years, I stuck to my scheduled exercise, ensuring I'd always be in a position to move fast while loving the energy and escapism running and parkour provided.

With the thought buzzing in my mind, it pushed me to pick up the pace. I was only doing five miles today—a luxury I afforded myself twice a week, half of my usual daily run. But fewer miles didn't mean I shouldn't push myself.

I turned right down Mason Street, forcing a burst of speed as I got closer to the small industrial part of town that I knew would be firmly closed up for the weekend. I closed in on a fast-approaching wall, opening myself up for the leap, the freedom. A few feet away, I launched, foot hitting the vertical wall, hauling up over it, and landing on my feet immediately as I sprinted toward the sign I knew could take me to the roof.

Warm air pushed against me as I leaped high, hand clamping around metal. I swung my legs up, feet touching the edge as I pushed hard, throwing myself forward into a roll before my sneakers scraped across the felt roof. Getting traction, I followed the path I knew so well. Two more strides and I flew, walking in the air, floating high for the barest of moments that felt like an eternity as my head cleared, the rush of adrenaline tingling through my limbs, stuttering my heart till I landed on the neighboring roof.

My hands barely found leverage as I rolled onto my soles, propelling forward.

My focus zeroed in on the next wall to the staggered buildings. I limbered myself, ready to find purchase, ready for impact. I jerked forward, flicked my head back and arched my spine simultaneously. My feet at a right-angle to the concrete wall lasted for the barest of moments as my legs followed my head, my taut body pinwheeling through the air. My feet landed on the roof, but I didn't pause as I spun, hurtling to my right.

Heart in my throat, mind alive with charged adrenaline, I fell eight feet, zeroing in on the metal bar waiting for me. The foothold stayed true, a slight shockwave echoing through my legs before I shoved off hard, somersaulted, and landed on the solid concrete.

I crouched low, my breathing heavy, labored with a burn of exquisite energy.

Allowing myself five seconds to breathe, to calm

my erratic heart, I smiled. Two breaths later, I pushed off at full pelt, limbs pumping and pushing furiously.

It wasn't until I was half a mile away that I slowed to a steady pace, no longer running as though the bats of hell were on my ass. The slower run kickstarted my brain, and immediately I zeroed in on thinking about Billy and the knowledge that he was waiting for me.

Yeah, something had definitely changed. And I still didn't know how to feel about that. Five miles did nothing to help me figure my head out.

Slowing to a stop at the front of the garage where my one-bedroom apartment was, I leaned forward, stretching, trying to psych myself up for spending time with the man.

Almost seven months ago, when he'd been buried balls deep in me, blowing my mind and soon after my load, I'd thought it had been the start of something. Our attraction had been immediate when I'd moved in over a year ago. It had burned brightly the months following, until the one night late after work I'd come home to find him sitting out front, drinking, and encouraging me to sit and chat. Two hours later, we'd ended up in a tangle of limbs and heat, following some of the best conversation I'd ever shared and leading to the most incredible sex I'd ever had.

All thoughts of something more had been quickly

erased the following morning when Billy had cussed at himself, then told me he was sorry and that him screwing me blind had been a mistake that would never be repeated and that he'd stay out of my way in the future.

A one-eighty hadn't come close to describing the change. The whiplash from his hot and heavy words as he'd all but worshipped my body to what he said the morning after had shattered the slightest hint of hope I'd had that he'd seen something in me that I'd struggled to see myself.

And that I was a mistake? Hell if that hadn't stung.

Five years it had taken me to have the courage to literally lay myself bare and open to another guy, only to have me quickly learning my lesson. It was totally me. His words to the contrary meant nothing.

And now he smiled and wanted to spend time with me again?

I shook my head. Screw that.

Making quick work of the external staircase, I opened the door, leaned in and swiped my skateboard and my wallet. I turned on my heel and headed away from his place, off the property, feet meeting wood. Just a few blocks would get me to the diner where I'd happily hide for a few hours.

Putting myself out there had tested every defense

I'd painstakingly put in place. He'd pulled them down and left me in tatters. It wasn't like I'd been left broken-hearted. It wasn't love that had been between us. Far from it. But being left and made to feel worthless was something I'd promised myself I'd never allow again.

Trusting him had been a mistake.

Billy now deciding he wanted something more, friends or maybe more than…. Well, it wasn't in me to lower my shields like that again. Not to someone who could potentially get inside and mean more.

I wasn't blind. He was hot, older for sure, but that was neither here nor there. And I honestly thought he was a good guy.

With a sigh, I pulled open the door to the corner diner that made half-decent coffee. Already I hesitated over my decision, brain and emotions at loggerheads and struggling. Maybe I could give friends a try if that were all he was after, I mused.

Frustration thrummed through me that Billy was stealing so much of my brainpower, and emotions to boot. But with little else going on in my life, there wasn't really anything else catching my focus.

I looked up at Marlene once I was settled in the booth and smiled. "Morning."

"You're here early," she said. "Needing a cup of the good stuff?"

"Absolutely." I turned my cup over and accepted the steaming black liquid with a relieved inhale. The scent immediately eased some of my tension.

"Having breakfast?"

I nodded. "Maybe in twenty."

"Sure thing, honey. Just give me a holler when you're ready to order." She turned and walked away, leaving a trail of lavender in her wake. While it didn't exactly go well with the coffee, the smell was familiar and comforting.

When I'd first arrived in Kirkby, and then here in Crescent, I'd been unsure of settling somewhere so small. The whole knowing almost everyone—if not names then at least faces—had taken time to get used to. And honestly, the friendly waves and genuine smiles from most residents had been hard to swallow.

The last thing I was used to was good people with no agendas. But a year on, I'd learned to trust it as best as I could. And over in Kirkby, the town where I worked, I felt even more comfortable. My position as bartender helped a lot. It meant I got to know people fairly well. Or as much as I allowed. Plus there were Ted and Jason, my bosses. They were nice, genuine. Ted was nosey as hell and interfered in everything whenever possible, but his heart was in a good place. The two of them had helped me get a place to live, even subbed me a month in advance rent at Billy's.

I trusted them implicitly. Though that didn't mean I'd been willing to share my life story with them. Some things were simply best left in the past.

A quick glance at the time told me it was almost seven. Town was slowly waking. Not that much was open at this time on a Saturday morning. The bakers, the coffee shop, this place, plus the small grocery store was pretty much it so far. But a few people milled around, taking dogs for a walk. A couple of parents with strollers and kids swinging off the side chattering away. It was peaceful, especially with just a few people already in the diner talking quietly over breakfast and coffee.

I eased back into the booth, finally relaxing. Stretching out my limbs a little, I exhaled, enjoying the gentle burn from pushing myself earlier.

Jumping around the place, charging up buildings, throwing myself off them was a vice from my teens I'd never shaken. Parkour did it for me. It was as simple as that. I rarely drank, didn't indulge in smokes or drugs; hell, beyond a few months back, I didn't even have sex. Or at least not often. Parkour offered me a release I craved. I needed the rush, the challenge to stay sane.

Back in one of the places I'd stayed, on the outskirts of Columbus, I'd run with a small crew, got up to adrenaline-fueled moves that would give most people nightmares. What I did these days was tame in comparison, mainly because being alone meant there was no one there to have my back. And while pushing myself was a helluva lot of fun, my edge had slipped. Twenty-seven didn't mean I was decrepit by any means, but I was more aware of my mortality.

When the door opened, I flicked my gaze to the two figures stepping into the diner. My smile was instant. While I didn't know Jasper all that well, nor his boyfriend, Austin, I'd met them last month at a dinner held at work. The whole get-together had been fun.

"Oh, hey," Jasper said, smiling brightly. "You want company?"

"Sure, go for it."

Jasper slipped in, Austin following as I said hi to him.

"Having breakfast?" Austin asked as he settled opposite, stretching his arm to rest behind Jasper's back.

"Just about to order. Just needed to inhale caffeine first."

"I hear you," Jasper said. "Not sure I'm actually

awake yet, but this guy here insisted." He raised his brow at Austin, who simply rolled his eyes.

"You said you wanted to get out early."

"Well, yeah," Jasper started, "but I was thinking maybe nine or something."

"It'll be too hot for our walk if we wait till later." Austin picked up the menu, casting a smile at his boyfriend.

I simply sat back and relaxed. They were both really nice guys. Austin was the principal at the local high school, and Jasper was a teacher.

"Any joy with a position?" I asked Jasper, recalling our conversation from last month.

"Yeah," he answered. "Just covering for a term of maternity leave."

"Excellent. Somewhere close?"

Jasper scrunched up his nose. "Sort of. I'm going to have to stay away during the week, maybe try to head home midweek so Austin here doesn't pine for me."

I cast a glance at Austin, who didn't look exactly pleased about this arrangement.

"It's only for three months," Jasper placated, leaning into Austin, having seen his reaction. "I'm hoping someone at Austin's school will get knocked up or something soon," he said with a laugh.

I snorted.

"Perhaps I need to organize weekend work retreats, partners welcome, and supply a heap of booze," Austin suggested. While there was humor in his voice, there was something in his eyes that suggested he was seriously considering the idea.

Jasper shook his head. "I don't think that's necessary. Something will come up."

Marlene appeared at the table, drawing our attention away. We gave our orders, and I happily accepted a refill. Once she'd left, Jasper refocused on me, eyeing my tee.

"You been out exercising this morning? Running, right?"

I bobbed my head. "Yeah. Five days a week."

His brows shot up. "Even when you have late nights at work?"

I shrugged. "Yeah. I wake up naturally early, so it's no effort, and if I need a nap or something, I just crash early or grab a power nap."

Jasper scrunched his nose, making me chuckle.

"Running is good for you. The body and the soul."

He didn't seem convinced and twisted his mouth. "I'll just take your word for it."

"You're making it sound like you don't do any exercise," Austin added.

"A long walk isn't running though." Jasper picked up his coffee and took a sip.

"True, but uphill today."

"Urgh. True," Jasper added. "We're heading out to one of the tracks out at Lanefield."

I racked my brain, trying to recall where he meant but ended up shrugging. "Not sure where that is."

Austin explained, "It's only about thirty minutes south of here. There are a few tracks. There's a nice walk through some forestry. Steep at times but nothing too strenuous."

"Sounds good. I'll check it out sometime." Despite my passion for running and parkour, I enjoyed exploring local trails, both for gentle walking and some harder hiking.

We continued to chat, and when our food was brought over, we dug in, laughing over the Christmas in July we'd all celebrated courtesy of Jason's visit from his sister who lived in Australia.

I headed to the restroom after eating and returned to both sets of eyes on me. "What?" I asked immediately, wondering if I'd missed something.

"We plan to head out to Lanesfield. We just need to pick up Penny but were wondering if you'd like to tag along?" Austin asked.

My eyes widened in surprise at their offer. "Oh,

wow, really? You don't mind me tagging along?" I was never quite sure with couples whether I'd end up being the third wheel or not.

Jasper was already shaking his head. "Of course not. We'd love to have you along. I mentioned to Billy a few times about asking you over to eat one night. He kept saying you were busy. Just thought it would be good to get to know each other better."

My stomach dipped, the taste in my mouth souring that Billy would do that. Not once had he ever extended the invite my way. One of Billy's jobs was working for Austin, looking after their dog, doing handyman stuff around the house, which he'd told me before it all went down seven months ago. There was another man, an older dude, who he did some hours for too. Sorta looked out for him, helped with groceries, hospital trips, and stuff.

I'd thought it was cool he did something low-key, especially when he'd shared some stories of the time when he worked as a cop. I didn't know why exactly he left, beyond an injury that damaged his leg.

"Yeah," I finally said, forcing a smile. "Shiftwork at the bar can be crazy, and trying to sort out a time that suits for dinners and get-togethers can be hard." There was some truth in my words, but I had more than enough evenings to myself that getting together was not a big deal at all.

"I get it. We'll definitely plan something soon though. But today, you game?" Jasper pushed.

I didn't even hesitate, despite the info about Billy slighting me. It beat hiding out in the diner all day. "Yeah, that sounds good. I'd love to, thanks."

"Great," Austin said, pulling out his wallet as he stood. I followed suit, leaving my payment on the table, along with a healthy tip for Marlene.

"Am I good to go like this? Do I need walking boots, or will my sneakers do the trick?" I prayed I'd be fine with what I wore. The last thing I wanted was to head home.

"I think you'll be fine. Most of the walk is under the shelter of trees too, so you should be good without a cap," Austin said.

Relief swept through me. Spending time with two good guys—made even better that they were a couple —at ease knowing friendship was all that was on offer, I relaxed, my shoulders settling.

I followed them to Austin's sweet old truck, grinning when I climbed in. "I know you've told me about how incredible your Ford is, but damn… she's sweet."

Austin smiled at me, and Jasper laughed. "That's all that's needed to get on Austin's good side, praising his baby." His smile was bright, voice filled with humor as we pulled away and headed toward their place—somewhere else I'd yet to visit.

I settled back, watching the world go by as we traveled to pick up their dog. Just maybe my bad day would turn out okay after all.

CHAPTER THREE

BILLY

THERE WAS NO DOUBT I DESERVED IT, BUT LAWRENCE running out on me without a heads-up still stung. The thing was, I couldn't challenge him, couldn't ask for an explanation, more than aware I'd lost that right a few months back.

Perhaps him not coming back after his run was a shit thing to do, but I wore the crown for that title, so I'd keep my mouth shut.

But I wouldn't give up.

Seven months of looking on from afar had been hard. I could have continued, reluctantly, painfully, giving a simple chin lift in greeting, shame and regret riding me hard, but after last month's get-together, Ted—the owner of the bar where the party was held— had planted a seed in my mind. The seed had sprouted, grown roots, and was determined to make me pull my head out of my backside where Lawrence was concerned—despite his silence and despite this latest development of him running away.

Seven months ago when I'd earned my title of asshole, I'd been in a seriously different place. While some elements had yet to resolve themselves, I'd come to terms that when I'd slammed on the brakes and refused to live my best life, it was an insult to Clark.

He'd give me hell and probably put hot sauce in everything I ate and drank for the foreseeable future if he knew I was so caught up with grieving that I'd stopped truly living.

I sighed. It was time to admit defeat. An hour and a half had passed by; Lawrence wasn't coming back anytime soon.

Rather than hanging around and sulking, I grabbed my wallet and keys and jumped in my car. The hardware store was the first destination.

Once there, I searched for colors, considering all I knew about Lawrence. While it was true we knew little about each other in the grand scheme of things, before my screwup, we'd chatted regularly and had begun to get an easy camaraderie going. It hadn't quite been friendship. Truthfully, I recognized the both of us had been too closed off for that, but with a little more time, I thought we could have got there.

Lawrence wore a lot of varying shades of blue. Whether he knew it or not, the color lit up his gray eyes something fierce.

They truly were piercing and were one of the first things I'd noticed about the guy when he'd come to look at the apartment.

Thinking about the apartment now, his space, his personal possessions, I realized there was very little around, or at least on display.

I hadn't spotted a single framed photograph. There was no artwork on the walls despite me giving him the go-ahead to do so. The furniture was mine, second-hand stuff mainly. Some of it could probably do with being replaced.

I hovered near the wall of colors, focusing on the blues and considering what variation to go for.

I knew what I liked, but I had no clue what would work or what his preference would be. Huffing out a breath, I debated what to do and tugged out my phone, trying not to overthink it.

Screw it.

I opened my contacts list, hit T, and scrolled till I found his name.

The call connected after three rings.

"And what do I owe the pleasure of this call?" Curiosity bled through Ted's words.

Rather than leading in and attempting polite, irrelevant conversation, I simply said, "Hi, Ted, I'm looking for paint to decorate the apartment."

"Lawrence's place?" he interrupted.

"Yeah."

"I see. Go on."

I rolled my eyes, sure he was lapping up the bizarreness of this call. "So I need to know what colors you think Lawrence would like. Can you help?"

He paused a beat before asking, "Is there a reason why Lawrence can't help you with this?"

Of course he asked that question, but I wouldn't be oversharing. "He's out for the day. I told him I'd be decorating and didn't get the chance to ask about color choices. I want to get a start though."

"Right, I see." And there was that all-telling amusement in his voice, with a silent "I call bullshit and know what you're up to." It had been exactly the same last month when he'd cornered me at the dinner party he and his husband had hosted.

After a few more questions, including me explaining which areas I'd be painting, which happened to be all of it, he finally gave me the goods. He followed up with texts containing links to color selections, along with a warning of **Do not screw this up!**

Needless to say, I knew he wasn't talking about my painting skills.

Armed with my purchases, including a new roller and a couple of brushes, I headed out, stopping by the diner to grab some takeout lasagna for my lunch. Once buckled into my car, I ran through my checklist to make sure I had everything. Realizing I was short of dust sheets, I flicked off a text to Austin, asking to borrow his.

He responded immediately, letting me know he was out and to help myself. I fired back my thanks and headed on over.

It was always strange being at Austin's house when his dog, Penny, wasn't home. She was the reason why'd I'd secured some work hours with Austin in the first place.

Once I was back on my feet post injuries, I'd made the drastic move to up and leave Chicago. The call for a quiet life beckoned, and this area with a small cluster of towns and the closest city just a few hours away sounded idyllic—and it was.

I had cash to settle myself in, didn't have a mort-gage, but I needed money for day-to-day living. I lived a simple life, so it wasn't like I needed a lot. When I'd spotted the ad for a dog sitter, I'd jumped at the chance. Hanging out with a dog rather than a human sounded like bliss.

It wasn't long into the job that I picked up more hours with Austin. He worked long days and was working on revamping his home and gardens. Since I'd always been handy, they were tasks I took on happily. Not long after, I also did some hours with Jacob, a veteran who lived on the outskirts of town and struggled to get around.

What I'd planned for as being perhaps a couple or three hours out of my day, pretty much turned into a full-time position between the two of them. It was all good. I enjoyed the work, enjoyed staying busy, plus the extra cash was nice. It meant I could do things like buy paint and a few new bits of furniture for the apartment above my garage.

I pulled the dust sheets out of the smaller shed, the much larger old brick shed having been recently converted to create a separate dwelling for Austin's brother, Frankie, and Frankie's son, Tyler.

A quick glance around the yard as I left alerted me that I could do with mowing the grass at some point this week, something I'd need to add to my list. As I stepped onto the driveway, I heard the crunch of gravel. My gaze landed on Austin's old Ford pickup. I smiled in greeting, my eyes darting to his side, seeing Jasper, and then I faltered slightly with my next step.

Lawrence was beside them.

My eyes remained glued to him. I saw the moment he spotted my car. A quick whip of his head followed, gaze landing on mine. His features blanched, making my gut dip. I hated that that was his immediate reaction to seeing me.

I continued to my car, placing the sheets in the trunk beside the paint. Once it was shut, I turned as the Ford stopped beside me, the engine cutting off.

Austin jumped out first, a smile on his mouth but concern in his eyes.

"Everything okay?" I asked immediately, flicking my attention to Lawrence, who remained seated, wondering why he wasn't simply getting out.

"Lawrence had a fall."

My gut plummeted for a whole different reason this time. Without considering my actions, I was at the passenger door, tugging the door open, my eyes roaming Lawrence, searching for injuries.

"What happened? You okay?" There was a small detachment to my voice as I assessed the situation, taking in as much of Lawrence as I could so I could work out what was needed. Cuts grazed his legs, a few trickles of blood seeming to have dried up. One sneaker was off, the swelling obvious, the bruising already at the surface. He cradled his wrist. I raked my gaze up to his face. Heat covered his cheeks, and surprise shot through me that he was looking right back at me, rather than avoiding all eye contact.

I'd seen enough broken limbs over the years to know it was likely a bone was fractured in his foot, maybe his ankle. While I was unsure about his wrist, there was enough pain in his eyes to let me know he was struggling.

And I didn't much like the cut on his head covered with dried blood. At least it was no longer flowing.

"I tried to take him to the hospital, but he just wanted to come here and get fixed up before I took him home," Austin said, his tone clearly frustrated.

"I really do think you need a hospital," Jasper added, his concern front and center.

I returned my attention to Lawrence, whose whole focus was on me. There was a new pleading there, a silent request for me to not push this, even though I knew a hospital was exactly what was needed.

When he said, "Billy, will you just take me home?" my chest tightened. He needed me, that much was absolutely obvious. But more than that, my years on the force told me there was more to this situation than Lawrence would like any of us to know.

Making a decision, I nodded, reaching in to help him out of the truck. "Austin, open the door, will you?"

He didn't hesitate in rushing over and pulling open the passenger-side door.

I stepped into the space between Lawrence and me. "Can you turn and move your legs out, careful of your foot?"

He nodded, still clutching his wrist. Moving carefully, Lawrence readjusted himself with no assistance from me, while I had my hands out and ready to help should he need me.

Penny started fussing in the back. "I'll get Penny inside," Jasper said. "I'll only be a minute." He exited from the driver side and dealt with the dog.

I lowered my voice, saying to Lawrence, "You okay if I help you out?"

His eyes met mine, and he bobbed his head.

With my hands on his waist, I edged him forward, trying to angle back as I did, not wanting him to catch his injured foot. "Let me take your weight."

Lawrence's lips were set in a thin white line, and he nodded, wincing as he did so. I lifted, ensuring I took the brunt of weight on my good leg. While we were similar in height—he was only maybe a couple of inches shorter—I was a little thicker set and bigger built. The extra weight and muscle that I hid beneath my plain clothes came in handy as I eased him to the ground on his good foot.

"I think if you hop, you're going to jolt yourself. Until you have some pain meds, that's the last thing you want."

A heavy huff of air left him before he inhaled a steady breath. Pain chased him something fierce if the tautness of his body and the paleness now in his face were anything to go by.

"Hold on to the door a second, then hold on to me with your good arm, okay?"

"Okay," he managed. My own breath escaped at that one word, relieved he was keeping himself together.

"I'll try my hardest to go steady, okay?"

"'Kay, thanks."

I moved to the side of him, bent my legs a little, and carefully scooped him into my arms. After a moment of becoming accustomed to his weight and allowing him to breathe through the grunt of pain that escaped, I took the few steps needed to get him into my car. Miraculously, I got him inside and buckled up without bouncing a limb off the vehicle. Relieved he was secure, I closed the door and faced Austin and Jasper, stepping toward them.

"What happened?"

Austin shook his head, a pissed-off expression crossing his features. "Dirt bikes out on the walking track. They appeared from nowhere, would have run over Penny, probably killed her with the speed if Lawrence hadn't got her out of the way." Anger rode him hard as he released a heavy breath.

Jasper reached out and wrapped an arm around his waist, his cheeks red and the same pissed-off expression on his face. "One ended up smashing into Lawrence. It was right next to an incline. Thank Christ it wasn't far down."

A heat of fury zipped through me. "The fuck?"

Jasper's jaw tightened. "The guy who hit him fell, then picked up his bike and rode out of there. At that point we just needed to get to Lawrence, make sure he was okay."

My jaw ached from gritting my teeth, wanting to find the shithead who'd hurt Lawrence. "Did he lose consciousness or anything?" I finally asked, a shake in my voice. "His head, the cut?"

"No." Austin shook his head. "But Billy," he leaned in, his voice dropping, "Lawrence freaked the hell out when I mentioned contacting the police and when I said he needed to go to the hospital." He cast a quick glance at his boyfriend, who gave a small nod. "I don't know. Something's just not quite okay. He seemed legitimately… I don't know, not frightened but definitely on edge."

I took that in, not quite sure how to respond but filing the information away. At the moment, making sure Lawrence was okay and would heal properly was my priority. After a beat, I said, "Okay. Thanks. I'll look after him and make sure he's all right."

Austin reached out and lightly gripped my arm. "I know you will. We're just worried."

"Me too." I glanced over my shoulder to check on Lawrence. His head was tilted back against the headrest, his eyes closed. "I need to get him home and settled." I stepped away, concern filling my limbs and making them heavy.

"Let us know he's okay," Jasper said as I reached for the door handle.

"Will do." I offered a tight smile, got in my car, and turned the engine over. "You let me know if you need anything on the way home, okay?" I said to the quiet man at my side.

The barest of head bobs was his response, which was good enough.

I headed home in silence, avoiding potholes and taking corners carefully. The whole way, my mind played over Lawrence and his reaction to receiving not only medical treatment but reporting the incident.

By the time I pulled up outside my house, a deep frown had creased between my brows. It was true I didn't know anything of significance about Lawrence's past, but if he was as on edge as Jasper and Austin had made out, there was more than his past to consider. That much anxiety or at least reluctance to treat broken limbs indicated that the past wasn't settled and there to stay.

I took a deep breath before I exited my car, knowing I had to decide just how far I was willing to push Lawrence on this.

He knew I used to be a cop, knew I'd become friendly-ish with the local sheriff, and clearly that hadn't been enough to have him running in the opposite direction. And that had me thinking: Was he actually running from something or someone?

CHAPTER FOUR

LAWRENCE

The cool water eased into my stomach. Gentle sips controlled enough to stop me from puking. This was not the first time I'd broken a bone, but it had been a few years since the last one. Parkour had resulted in seven breaks in total, and each time I'd dealt with it as low-key as I could.

"There's something definitely broken in your foot." The gentlest of touches coincided with Billy's words. "You need to have an X-ray in case it's not set right."

I swallowed the last of the liquid, holding my injured wrist still. "I'm sure it'll be fine. A moon boot or strapping should do the trick." Paranoia had chased me over the years. It was a hard feeling to shake and an almost impossible habit to break—the need to remain incognito.

But even more so now was my desire to remain under the radar so I could settle and call this place home.

Billy's silence, his tender hold on my foot had me looking at him. His gaze remained set on me. Not challenging exactly, more assessing.

"How many days a week do you run?" he asked, his tone without inflection.

I clenched my jaw, understanding exactly where he was going with this.

"If this sets wrong, you'll be lucky to jog the distance of the street."

I looked at the empty glass, defeat an ugly feeling.

"Are you going to be safe going to the hospital? Your name in the system going to send alarm bells ringing?"

I jerked my gaze up, making eye contact, reminding myself that he'd been a cop in a busy city before this. A detective even. With a huff of breath, I moved my head from side to side in the barest of movements. My pounding head wouldn't allow for anything more. "No. There won't be a SWAT team or anything dashing in." Rolling my eyes wasn't an option, but I was sure my tone did the job.

His mouth quirked, and the butterflies that were regularly around in his presence took flight in my stomach. "Well, that's good to know. I really think you need X-rays. If there's no alternative, we'll figure something out, but I don't want you to damage yourself for good or anything."

His words had my breath hitching as I absorbed them. My brows dipped low as I said, "You'd do that, help me find out another way?"

"Absolutely. If there's a reason you can't go to the hospital, I'll think of something else."

A flurry of emotion danced around in my chest. The last thing I wanted was to be indebted to anyone, especially the man who'd rocked my world only to dismiss me. "Why?" I asked. I seriously needed to know.

He didn't shrug, nor did he shy away when he answered, "I think you need help and I can give it to you. I want to give it to you," he clarified. "Honestly, I want to get to know you better."

Wide-eyed at his honesty, the question of what happened all those months ago burned in my throat. Asking that, without any guarantee of what his answer would be, was too much for now. Already I felt vulnerable. Not only did my foot and wrist throb, but my head stung and threatened to explode, and the cuts and scrapes stung something fierce.

As if sensing my inner battle, he said, "Listen, I am

sorry about what happened… before." His jaw clenched at the words, an emotion flashing in his eyes that I couldn't read. "I wasn't in a great place, and I'm just now trying to sort my own shit out. I pushed you away in the worst possible way—"

"The shittiest," I added, cutting him off, finally finding my voice and the confidence to speak up. This wasn't the first apology he'd given, but with my ego hurt after his brush-off, I hadn't been in the right place to accept it.

His lips tilted high, the movement sending those damn wings crazy. "The shittiest," he agreed. "I want to help you and get to know you in whatever way you'll let me. What do you say?" A small shrug followed, the first hint of uncertainty I'd seen from him.

I tilted my head back, wincing at the pull, the bump forming on my head reminding me it was probably best I shouldn't ignore my injuries. Heading to the hospital wasn't going to put me at risk. Intellectually I knew that, but despite both time and distance, some habits were hard to break.

Looking back at Billy, who remained crouched at my feet, hand still touching me, I said, "Okay. I could probably do with getting my head checked out."

His face contorted, brows dipping, face flushing, mouth pulling in tight. His words were eerily calm when he asked, "From the cut on your temple?"

I was sure that tone could make men cower in their boots, but hell if a ripple of awareness didn't race through me. A throb of pain quickly followed, reminding me now was so not the time to react to the alpha vibe all but pouring off Billy.

"Well, yeah, but I think I hit it pretty hard at the back," I admitted, curious for his reaction. I'd met plenty of tough guys in my time, some even cops, but Billy was something else. Just a little taller than me, at first glance he'd seemed fit. But that night I'd seen him without his clothes revealed the muscle he was packing. It left little doubt that when he'd carried me earlier, he could have done so for a lot longer than seven steps without breaking a sweat. But he wasn't like any cop I'd previously met—in as much as all the police I'd met over the years didn't look or speak like Billy.

Classically handsome, he pulled off a five o'clock shadow as well as a cleanly shaved face. And under his good looks, there was this careful control almost buzzing off him. When he smiled, he was all warmth and friendliness. But too many times—mainly after our night together—his smile had been rare. A strange, fierce calm radiated off him. It set my nerve endings alight while making me feel safe.

It was weird as hell.

And I was nothing like him at all. Heck, I lived for the "just out of bed" look, and rarely shaved unless my bristle annoyed me too much.

Billy's eyes closed for a moment, certainly longer than a blink, the second tell that he was struggling. Keeping my mouth shut, I waited, still mesmerized by his reaction.

After a couple of beats, his eyes sprang open, and he stood, carefully removing his hand. I frowned, feeling the loss, almost mourning it. Confusion alongside the pulsing pain felt like shit. My draw toward Billy had remained constant. It had grown within the first few months of getting to know him, and after we'd hooked up, I'd tried my hardest to dismiss him, push all thoughts and feeling for the man away, but I'd known I'd failed.

Attraction was one thing, but this Billy, who cared in a way that seemed above that of a landlord, flipped my emotions over, creating a flashing danger sign as it sent my heart into overdrive.

"Come on." His hands were on me and he helped me stand. "Arm," he instructed.

"Don't you want to get the doors if you're being all chivalrous and shit?" I asked, injecting humor in this situation, trying to cut through the weird tension.

He quirked his brow at me. In the process, the severity of the expression dropped away, easing some of the pressure in my chest and his shoulders.

A heavy sigh escaped his lips. "I suppose. Can you balance?"

"As long as you don't take long."

"I'll be back." His gaze swept over me, as if checking I could really manage to stay upright.

My lips quirked. "I'm fine, Arnie, geez."

His snort took me by surprise, the sound pleasant and making a full smile form on my face.

"Okay, smartass."

He was gone, opening the door and heading outside while I remained on one foot, good hand resting on the back of the armchair. Barely any time had passed before he was back and I was in his arms.

This time I had a new appreciation for being in this position. It didn't mean I'd stopped hurting like hell, but something had flipped in the albeit brief conversation we'd had.

Held securely in his strong arms, I realized that despite our history, I trusted Billy. Maybe not with my heart, but enough for him to care for me and have my back.

AFTER SIX HOURS, MY LEFT FOOT IN A MOON BOOT, MY right arm in a cast, tape on my temple, and no sign of concussion, I sat on Billy's comfy couch, feet propped on a soft footstool, eating a slice of pizza.

The thought of food hadn't even crossed my mind until Billy had set me up in his sitting room—with little argument from me. The thought of climbing the staircase to my apartment had made me shudder. Once settled, he'd offered to make me food. My "no thanks" had been punctuated by my growling stomach.

He'd simply smiled, got me a glass of water, given me pain meds, and returned not long after with what looked like homemade pizza. And damn if it wasn't the best pizza I'd ever had.

"Just saying, pineapple on pizza makes me want to hurl," he said, throwing a look of disbelief my way. "Whoever came up with the concept was a sadist."

I snorted, chewing around the mouthful of pepperoni and peppers I'd been all but inhaling. After swallowing, I laughed, saying, "Hey, I didn't say I like it. It was just a question."

"Thank Christ for that," he said, grinning. "Not sure I could cope forming this friendship if that were the case."

I tilted my head, my brain no longer pounding thanks to the strong drugs working their way through my system. "Is that what this is?" I asked, not quite sure I'd usually ask a question quite so blunt without the fuzziness in my brain. "Friendship?" I clarified, silently praising the pharmaceutical companies for making such fine drugs that were well on the way to making me speak my mind, consequences be damned.

Billy took a deep drink of his own water, eyes intent on mine before he placed the glass down. "I'd really like to get to know you better. Friends would be a great start." His words were clear, confident, voice holding an edge of determination I'd never heard before.

I squinted, actually thought I closed one eye to try to make my brain work things out a bit better.

"You okay?" Concern laced his words.

"Yeah, this is my thinking face," I said, wondering why my voice sounded so dreamy. It was kinda cool.

Billy pulled his lips between his teeth, his cheek-bones popping at the movement. "And what are you thinking?" he finally asked, his mouth twitching as he spoke.

What was I thinking?

I thought he was pretty, in a handsome, stern way. When he'd got all serious earlier, I'd almost sprung a hard-on, and what I knew about the man I liked a lot. "I almost moved out," I ended up saying. My eyes widened in surprise, wondering where those words came from, as they were not what I'd been thinking at all.

His expression shuttered a moment until it morphed into understanding, perhaps guilt, and what I liked to think was regret.

"But you didn't."

"Nope," I answered, popping the *p*. "It's quiet here. Feel safe. Settled." I shrugged and took another bite of my pizza. "And thank God, as this pizza is epic," I said around a mouthful of food. I shot him a closed-mouthed grin before closing my eyes and savoring every chew and liking the way my bones relaxed. "Can bones go melty? I think mine have melted." I snorted. "It's nice."

He didn't answer immediately, but that was okay. I had this pizza. It was great company. I tilted my head back, pressing against the cushion, chewing happily and smiling as I did so. The sound of movement had me lazily opening one eye.

Billy was returning from the kitchen. I hadn't even realized he'd left.

"I've just made the bed in the spare room, so let's get you washed up and asleep."

Sleep sounded good. But there was pizza. I looked down and frowned. My plate had gone. Confused, I looked around. "Where'd my pizza go?" My pizza abandoning me was so not okay.

"You finished, I took the plate, got things set up, and just woke you."

I scrunched my nose. "I wasn't sleeping."

"Right, okay. The freight train sound is a normal part of everyday breathing, huh?"

My mouth gaped. "I do not snore."

"You're right. That's beyond any snore I've heard before. It could come with its own name." His mouth twitched again. I was sure that had happened a few times since being here.

"But I'm injured... and you're teasing," I grumped, finding myself half serious until his lips turned into a full-on smile. There went my melty bones again. I liked it a lot when he smiled, apparently. It had enough power to wipe away my drug-induced complaint. "I like it when you do that thing with your mouth at me."

A wide yawn followed, and my eyes drifted to half-mast. "I can sleep here."

He was in front of me before I could fully close my eyes, pulling me up, cradling me in his arms again, and taking me to what I assumed was his spare room.

"I'll let you pee first. We can figure out showering tomorrow." His voice was quiet, barely touching my brain as I snuggled against his broad chest.

"I could pee." My eyes were closed as I spoke, my words increasingly slurry. This whole thing was weird. My fuzziness was a bit like being drunk, but it was like looking down on myself, a hazy awareness of my words and actions swirling through my mind.

Before I knew it, I'd peed, washed my hands and face, and then had been tucked into bed.

I opened my eyes when the bedside lamp was switched off, and the gentlest of touches smoothed back my hair. Billy peered down at me. Not too close to make me jump or worry he was being weird, though the thought made me smile. "Can't remember the last time anyone tucked me in," I whispered sleepily into the darkness.

Half in shadow, due to the light spilling in from the open doorway, Billy remained quiet, his hand now still but remaining in my hair.

"It's nice. Night, Billy."

One more gentle caress followed. My happy sigh filled the room at the touch. His whispered words of "Night, Lawrence" followed before he stepped away, propping my door open a crack and leaving me to fall asleep feeling wonderfully content and safe.

CHAPTER FIVE

BILLY

Somehow I managed to sleep, despite being aware of every sound in the house, vigilant of listening out for the man in my spare room.

Yesterday had been a whirlwind from the moment I'd realized Lawrence was injured. I'd gone into hyperdrive, ensuring he was cared for and safe, making sure he was looked after properly at the ER. The whole time, I'd observed him closely, checking he was really okay with being at the hospital. With Jasper and Austin describing Lawrence's reaction, I wanted to be certain I could jump on any potential issue.

Thankfully, there wasn't one.

We'd spent around six hours or so together yesterday before I'd brought him home. In that time, I'd distracted him from his discomfort as much as possible. This meant I'd seriously talked myself into exhaustion. These days I was used to spending time by myself or with a dog, and so many full-on hours of talking about largely insignificant topics was probably the reason why I'd managed to get some shut-eye despite my worry.

Relieved it was Sunday so I didn't have to dash out to see Jacob, I didn't race out of bed. It was only early. The dawn sun remained low in the sky, but still bright enough to light up my room.

Other than a few birds fluttering around outside singing, there was a stillness and quietness to the day that calmed me. I'd have a whole day to make plans and figure out exactly what Lawrence needed, but right now, I appreciated the gentle breeze nudging my curtains.

While Lawrence had been high last night, the conversation we'd had was important. I could only hope he remembered it. We hadn't truly got everything out in the open, and I didn't think anytime soon was right for it either. But I'd been honest about wanting friendship.

More would be awesome too, but jumping from a one-night stand to where we were now had already taken its toll. I could be and would be patient, but more than that, I'd work at being his friend and getting to know him better.

With both of the bedroom doors open, I heard the creak of a mattress, followed by a groan and a "Shit!"

Perhaps I shouldn't have grinned, figuring he'd probably knocked one of his broken limbs, but the man made me smile, and hearing his voice in my house was kinda nice.

I climbed out of bed, needing a piss, but realizing I'd better check on Lawrence first. He was pretty much incapacitated with the nature of his injuries. It would mean the next few weeks would be a serious ball ache for the guy.

I gave a couple of knocks on his open doorway, waited a beat, then entered. "Morning. How're you doing in here?"

A more natural color filled Lawrence's face this morning, a relief to see. He was sitting up, sheet pooled around his waist, chest unfortunately not exposed, but he looked less out of it.

"Hey," he said. He cracked his neck from side to side, wincing as he did so. "I feel like I've been hit by a bike." He flicked his gaze at me and offered a small smile. I smirked back in response.

"Is it bad if I say you look like you have too?"

His smile widened, and he chuckled. "That would be a terrible thing to say."

I nodded. "In that case, you look incredible, refreshed even. You been on vacation recently?"

He rolled his eyes at me, reached out with his good arm, and tugged at the sheet to expose his legs. "I really need to piss," he said. He threw me an apologetic smile. "This is gonna be a nightmare, isn't it?" He frowned at his leg and his arm, both breaks on different sides of his body.

"It's not going to be the best, for sure," I said. "Skateboarding days may be numbered for a while." My heart went out for the guy. Yesterday when I'd challenged him to get him to agree to head to the hospital, I'd played on his passion for running. I hoped this wouldn't wreck things for him. "The doc said the breaks were super clean though. Being careful now, then gradual exercise will get you up and running in no time." I stepped toward him as I spoke so I could reach for him and take him to the bathroom. "We might need to grab a wheelchair or one of those kneel wheelie things." I had no idea of the correct term, but I'd seen a couple of people around town with a weird scooter they kneeled on.

There was something strangely ordinary, comforting almost about Lawrence being in my arms.

Wordlessly, ensuring I didn't blurt that information out, I headed to the bathroom and settled him down. "You good for a few minutes while I get myself together?"

He steadied himself, hand on the basin. "Absolutely. Thanks."

I nodded and hesitated near the door. "Just don't try to be a hero and start hopping or some shit, all right?" Seriously, the last thing he needed was another fall.

A shy smile crossed his mouth. "Okay. I'll wait for you."

My concern settling at his words, I bobbed my head again and closed the door behind me so I could head to my en suite bathroom.

I raced through getting cleaned up and threw on some fresh clothes, moving as quickly as possible. I returned to the bathroom, knocking on the door. "All good for me to come in?"

"Yeah."

I pushed open the door and struggled to not groan. He'd managed to pull off his tee, exposing his sculpted chest and back. While the guy wasn't built, he was fit and looked delicious. Dragging my gaze away from his lickable skin, my eyes snagged on his through the mirror's reflection. His brows were high, and amusement danced in his eyes. I simply shrugged, having no shame in being caught ogling.

"You all finished here or need a hand with anything?" My voice was a lot deeper than I'd intended.

"I think I'm done." He turned, and I stepped further into the bathroom.

"I'll get you on the couch, then go and grab you some clean clothes if that's okay?"

"That'd be great." He grunted a little as I picked him up.

"Did I hurt you?" Concern laced my words.

"I'll live. And as much as I like being manhandled by you, this really is going to frustrate the hell out of me, and definitely you."

"I get it," I said, reaching the couch and lowering him down. "And I promise we'll sort something to get you mobile. You heard what the doc said about not hopping around just yet, right?"

He bobbed his head, still looking a little disgruntled. "Yeah. I heard, and I have no plans to do more damage."

Happy with his response, I smiled. "Let me get the coffee on, then I'll head to your place. Anything you need in particular?"

"My phone charger, just clean underwear, shorts, and a tee is great. Oh, my toothbrush and deodorant."

"You got it."

I passed him the TV remote before heading to the kitchen to start a fresh pot of coffee. I then grabbed the keys to his apartment and made my way to the door. Before I stepped outside, Lawrence's voice stopped me.

"I really appreciate you doing this for me." His voice was quiet but steady, his eyes on me when I looked back at him. "Thank you."

Heat spread through me. "I'm glad I can help. It's all good." I threw him a wink and headed on out.

After sorting Lawrence's clothes, the morning continued in making calls, trying to find access to a wheelchair or one of those kneeling scooters. As I organized that, Lawrence made a call to Jason, letting him know what had happened, and that he'd need some time off work.

Finally solving the mobility problem with a call to Austin, after a range of calls trying to track something down, I came off the phone smiling. Lawrence's frown had my grin slipping, however. "What's wrong?" I asked, heading toward him. "You in pain? Need some meds?"

He jumped a little when I spoke, his eyes roaming

over my face. He'd clearly been distracted and was trying to catch up. "Oh, no. I'm fine. No pain. Bit of a headache that I can ignore. Some aches, but all good."

I nodded, relieved that was the case. But that didn't explain away his dipped brows. "Good, so what's wrong? Why the face?"

He huffed out a breath and closed his eyes briefly before looking back at me. I knew a defeated look when I saw one. With almost twenty years as a cop, I'd learned quickly how to read people.

"Whatever's wrong, we can figure it out," I said, trying to reassure him. I felt sorry for the guy. One broken bone was one thing, but two, preventing him from using crutches, was a nightmare. Even if he wasn't injured though, I'd already decided I wanted to get to know him properly, try to change the course of our relationship. Even if that only led to friendship. "So why not just share and we'll see what we can do?"

Lawrence seemed to mull it over, the whole time studying me. After a few beats, he said, "I've got some cash in savings that should cover me for a while, but I'm not sure when I can go back to work." His mouth twisted, and a hint of pink crawled its way up his neck.

Disliking his embarrassment, I interrupted, needing to reassure him. "Don't sweat it. I'm not worried about you paying rent on the apartment. Keep your savings."

He shook his head. "No, I wasn't saying I couldn't pay, just—"

"I know, but let me do this for you. Truth is, it looks like you're stuck in my spare room for a while, so it's not like you're going to be using the apartment or anything. When you're back to work, we can go back to normal, but there won't be a need to backdate or anything."

His expression was stoic, all except his eyes, which gave so much away. I understood his struggle. I didn't say any more, recognizing his need to process my offer. Finally, his shoulders sagged a little, his eyes zeroing in on mine. "Why are you doing this?" There was no accusation in his voice, no bite. The question was quiet, curious.

I answered honestly, "Shit happens, and when it does, it's important we help each other whenever we can." I sat on the footstool before him, careful of his injury. "This world can be a pile of horse dung." I shook my head, knowing all too well just what a pile it could be. "But along the way, I've had a couple of people stick their neck out for me, give me a helping hand when I needed it. Sometimes it seemed like something so small and insignificant, yet it ended up being life changing—others have saved my life. This is me being a good guy and doing the right thing." My fingers flexed, eager to reach out and touch his hand, provide that additional level of comfort and connection. But I held back. Without a doubt I wanted more with Lawrence, but I would not confuse my offer with my attraction to him.

He deserved better than that.

With his head tilted to the side as he studied me, Lawrence's words took me by surprise. "I'm glad I didn't move out."

"Wasn't sure if you'd remember yesterday with all of the painkillers in your system."

His lips tilted a fraction. "I remember, and I'm not simply glad because you're helping me out, no matter how much I appreciate it."

"You're not?" Curiosity had my voice lifting.

"No." He shook his head. "I think you were an asshole but had your reasons." His voice was so matter-of-fact that it drew a snort from me.

"I did." I paused before saying, "And I *am* sorry."

"I believe you."

I huffed out a breath and didn't attempt to hide my relief at his words. A small chuckle followed. "Shit, it's like story hour flipped to honesty hour or something right now." I carded my fingers through my hair, trying to shake off the feelings racing through me. Yeah, I was relieved, but the hope that chased that emotion was alien, making me feel vulnerable in a way that I hadn't in a long time.

After a moment, he responded. "Perhaps one day soon, if we're working on this friendship you offered, we can talk about it some more."

I bobbed my head, willing us to reach the point where we could share naturally and openly. But for the moment, this would be enough. "We can do that," I offered. "But for now, let me head out and grab this scooter thing." I reached out and placed my hand on his that rested on his thigh. I didn't linger after the small squeeze I offered.

I stood and then considered the best thing for Lawrence. "How about I drop you off at Austin and Jasper's while I'm out? At least that way you have some help."

"Yeah, that sounds great, thanks."

"Great. Let me give them a quick call and get this show on the road then."

As I carried him out to the car, fully aware I was giving my leg a workout it hadn't received in a while, I hoped that me sharing some of my past when the time came would open the door to the mystery that was Lawrence.

CHAPTER SIX

THERE WAS NO WAY I COULD HAVE GOT THROUGH THE past few weeks without Billy. That first week especially. While I'd turned his world upside down, not once did he complain or appear put out. Instead, he took it all in stride, with his main mission ensuring I was at ease and showing me care I couldn't remember ever experiencing before—well, not since before my dad passed.

This past week sped by with me whizzing around on the mobility scooter to the point where I was sure I was going to give Billy a heart attack. Each skid to a halt I made before running into something gave me a surge of adrenaline my body craved, with an extra kick of something for eliciting a reaction from the guy. I had to admit, getting a rise out of him was kinda fun.

Billy had managed to spend most of the first week at home. With it being the last week before Austin and Jasper went back to work, he didn't need to be around their place to look after their dog and whatever else he did with his working day. While he'd had a list of tasks to do, apparently nothing was urgent that couldn't wait. He'd been out to visit Jacob, the old man I knew he helped out. Once he let me tag along since it was clear I was going stir-crazy staying indoors.

The entire week had been the two of us settling into a weird and strangely comfortable routine while I got to know Billy on a whole new level.

Since then, we'd struck up a new schedule. He went to work but only usually for a few short hours a day. Apparently he hadn't been needed so much around Austin's with Frankie, his brother, living there. Meanwhile, I'd been going through the motions, slowly going insane, and bored out of my mind.

Though the time hadn't been a complete loss.

A couple times, Billy had dropped me off at the bar so I could cause mischief there, and in the afternoons when Billy was back, we'd been working on decorating the apartment. Plus, the forced proximity had meant I'd spent a lot of time with Billy and getting to know the man.

Over the past few weeks, I'd learned that eggs made Billy gag. He'd happily eat his weight in cakes and noodles, but crack an egg open and cook that up in a way where it was clear you were eating an egg, and his face took on an interesting shade of pale green. He was the youngest of three brothers, both were still cops, and his parents had not long celebrated their forty-seventh wedding anniversary.

The description of the party the family had thrown his parents for their forty-fifth celebration had me laughing and wondering what it would be like to have so much love and support in my life.

The discovery that he used to be into jumping out of planes and bungy jumping made me pause. We'd just finished eating the steak and salad we'd thrown together when he dropped that bombshell on me.

"You're shittin' me, right?" Billy was fit, built under the shirts that never clung, an ex-cop… the latter had taken me some time to get my head around when I'd first discovered it over a year back, but the more I knew of him, the more I'd seen snippets of his professional self.

But this did not match the image I had of the guy at all.

His laughter was loud. "I shit you not."

"But when, where, why?" The words spilled out as I tried to piece together who this man was.

He leaned back on the dining room chair, pushing his plate away. An easy smile settled on his lips. "The first time was in college. After that, I was hooked. Did a few base jumps too. They were a rush like you wouldn't believe."

I shook my head, nonplussed. "Seriously, who are you?" I was dead-set serious, but wonder filled my voice.

He quirked his brow at my question. "Do I not seem like the guy who chases a rush every now and then?"

"You seem like a lot of things," I said honestly. "Controlled, serious with a playful side that few get the chance to see. Ordered."

His smile slipped a little. While it didn't disappear completely, there was a sadness to this smile. I'd seen it before, and every time I had, it moved me. The sadness spoke to my soul, and, beyond reaching out and holding him, I had no idea what to do with my reaction. Instead of pulling him to me, knowing for sure that was not the direction I should be taking, I simply waited, watching and wondering how he'd respond.

"I think you've got me all figured out," he said, a gentle curve to his lips. "I can't even argue with anything you said."

"I don't think there's anything wrong with what I just described," I added quickly.

His gaze softened at my words, easing my thumping heart a little. The last thing I wanted was to offend the man.

"So, tell me about some of the places you've been, jumps you've made."

"Yeah?" His softening gaze morphed into a lightness I'd yet to witness before. "You really interested?"

My "Yes" perhaps came out too fast, too gravelly, but damn was I interested. I swallowed hard, not wanting to make this moment more than it was: the two of us simply getting to know each other better.

"Hell...." He swiped his hand through his brown hair, something I'd noticed he did when he got either excited or even a little nervous. "The last time I did anything like it was nearly four years ago."

"Oh, wow, so long?"

"Yeah. But that was when I headed to Anchorage in Alaska." My eyes widened in surprise while I also filed away the fact that he didn't want to touch on why he hadn't been skydiving or anything like it in so long. "It was intense. Did some decent freefalling there. Plus, you know, the scenery wasn't half bad." He followed through with a wink, his face becoming animated as he continued, "The glaciers from up there were just—" He shook his head, eyes unfocused. "Spectacular. Must admit there was something different being surrounded by snow and ice. It seemed more intense yet peaceful somehow. Serene, almost."

His eyes refocused on me, and I smiled widely at how happy he seemed, lost in the memory.

"It sounds awesome."

"It was."

"Well, if you ever decide to head back, feel free to hook a guy up." And I was deadly serious. I'd never had the cash to do something like skydiving before, but once I was fixed up, I could definitely start saving for that adventure specifically.

"Yeah? You ever done it before?"

"No." I shook my head. "But it's on my bucket list. I worry it could be an obsession I can't afford though," I said with a laugh.

"I hear you. I have my own kit, which helps, but still, securing a plane and pilot doesn't come cheap, you know?"

"I can imagine." I took a gulp of my water when he stood up and took hold of my plate. "Thanks," I said.

He offered me a relaxed smile. "No problem," he said, heading to the dishwasher.

"I can fill that up," I said, starting to stand, only to stop when he said, "I've got it. You've probably pushed yourself today already as it is."

I sighed and sat back down, reluctantly knowing he was right. Yesterday and today I'd insisted on helping with the painting in my apartment. It had meant navigating up the staircase, which was ridiculously exhausting, and then sitting on my ass with a paintbrush or a roller. That I was so exhausted pissed me off something fierce. "Thanks," I answered.

"Don't sweat it. Your energy levels will be back in no time." He threw me a smile of reassurance, and I grasped on to it, hoping he was right. "So, you're really up for a jump?"

I nodded enthusiastically. "Damn straight. Can't beat an adrenaline rush. Christ knows how I'm going to survive the next few weeks without one."

A questioning frown had his brows dipping low as he made his way back to the table. "Running?" he asked, sitting down opposite me.

Heat spread across my cheeks, and honestly, I had no idea why, beyond me never really discussing how I lived for parkour. I supposed, in the past, I'd received derisive comments, especially once I'd become an adult. "Well, there's my running for sure. Keeping in shape is important, and I do love it." I made sure I made eye contact when I said, "But I also do parkour," curious for his reaction.

His eyes widened at that. "Here? In town?"

I laughed at his disbelief, recognizing our small town certainly didn't scream of adrenaline junkies and people pushing themselves to their limits. "Yeah, here. I head out toward the small industrial part of town, close to where Jackson's Cabinetry is."

"Yeah, I know the place."

"Well, there's about twenty units or so, a bunch of opportunities really that are ideal."

"Holy shit, okay." He tilted his head, something shifting in his attention on me, but I wasn't sure exactly what that was. "And you do it by yourself?" This time concern lifted his words.

I nodded. "Yeah. I don't push it too far though. I know my limits."

He seemed relieved by that, his shoulders relaxing. "I suppose I understand more why you thought you could take on a dirt bike." There was a little sass in his words that had me smirking.

"Maybe," I answered, more than aware this was the first time we'd discussed the incident. There was clear hesitation, a silent pause where I just knew he was wondering about my reaction to being hurt. At the time, I'd had a freak-out, embarrassingly, and honestly unnecessarily so. I just wondered if he would ask me about it now.

When he didn't say anything more beyond, "When you're back up and running, I'd love to come out and watch you some time," not only did surprise flutter through me, but also a new respect that he recognized I didn't want to be pushed.

Our gazes connected, and I bobbed my head, answering honestly, "I'd really like that too."

His returning smile had my heart flipping over itself, liking far too much that it was directed at me. As he reached out for his glass, he asked, "Do you want to go outside on the porch? Looks like the temperature should have dropped enough for it to be pleasant."

Despite this feeling almost like date-like territory, there was nothing I wanted more. "Sounds good." I reached for my scooter and kneeled on my leg with the ankle break, good foot flat on the ground.

"I'll get our drinks, and let me get the door too." He took our glasses and led the way, escorting me outside. I reached the comfortable outside furniture and sat down, sinking into the softness of the seating.

The sun was in the process of setting, pretty purple tinting the sky. It was still too light for the fireflies, but a few crickets called in the distance. I looked up, only a couple of stars visible in the fading light. It wouldn't take long for that to change though. It never did. There wasn't a great deal of light pollution around, but here at Billy's house, just on the edge of town, the stars were more visible than anywhere else I'd lived before.

Billy's soothing voice startled me. "I love this time at night." I glanced over at him. His eyes were focused on the distance, much like mine had been a moment ago. "I love it when the stars are bright in the sky, but when there's still some light visible, I don't know, there's something about it."

"Yeah," I said quietly, something about the moment having me lower my voice. "Peaceful. Like possibility."

At my words, he turned and captured my gaze. Intensity filled his eyes, a flicker of understanding as he nodded. "It just helps to settle the shit in my head."

Those were the most honest words he'd ever spoken to me, and from the flaring of his eyes, I figured he knew that as much as I did.

"Mine too." I wanted him to know I felt it, understood how messed up life could be. But with that reality came possibility. "And all because of a pretty sunset," I added with a smile, wanting to lighten the moment but not erase it. "Who'd think it possible, right?"

Billy returned my smile, the curve of his lips becoming one of my favorite sights. "It's good that it's possible." After a beat, he flicked his focus away, once more staring into the distance.

We sat that way for the rest of the night, exchanging quiet conversation, and me explaining how I'd first got into parkour, without delving into my life story. Just maybe I'd open up to Billy when the time was right, if our friendship stayed strong, but it wasn't right now under the summer sky and the dancing stars.

THE NEXT MORNING, I DRAGGED MYSELF OUT OF BED, got washed up, and headed to the kitchen to have breakfast. Billy had already left. He'd let me know last night he'd be leaving early to get on with some chores and such.

I spooned my cereal to my mouth, barely stopping for breath. I really wanted to get a start on the day and get on with the painting.

My ankle and wrist were both in the early stages of healing. I'd had enough broken bones over the years, mainly from hitting the ground just on the wrong side when bouncing around the streets doing parkour, that

I understood my limits. As such, I knew what my body could handle.

The break in my ankle was clean, making it much easier to hobble about in my moon boot, but I made sure to stay off it regularly. My wrist was frustrating, but I could move my fingers, and the ER doc had told me doing so would be fine, on the proviso I didn't overdo it.

And while being an invalid sucked, I was far from being a teenager, so knew not to push it too far.

Once I'd washed up my breakfast bowl, I scooted outside and made it to the bottom of the steps of the garage. Once there, I shifted onto my ass and butt shuffled the way to the top, one slow step at a time. A couple of days ago, I'd managed to hobble up on one good foot and my boot, but I'd been clumsy, to the point I'd thought Billy was going to blow a gasket. After that, I promised Billy I wouldn't try again without him. At least until I could take more weight on my injured foot.

Before long, I'd organized the paint needed. My plan was to tackle my bedroom. The room had already been cleared to allow me to move around easily, and Billy had put a chair and a high stool in the room to help me too.

I smiled at the thought. He always appeared to be

one step ahead, anticipating my needs. It was kind of sweet, albeit a bit surreal.

It didn't take long before I found my rhythm cutting in, then followed through with a roller. Just as I made to dip my paintbrush into the can to start on the edges of the doorframe, my cell rang. I made quick work of placing the brush down before limping over to the windowsill where I'd left my phone. I glanced at the name before answering with a smile and a "Hey, Ted."

"Oh, my sweet melon dew. How are you?"

I laughed at his greeting, never quite sure what would come out of his mouth. "I'm great. How're you and Jason? Everything okay?"

"Yes, yes, don't worry about us, we're both fine. Surviving without you, just. But you need to hurry up and recover. Sharing too many shifts with Sherry is going to drive me to distraction."

I snorted in understanding. Sherry was a part-timer. She was sweet, middle-aged, and was as unusual as she was fabulous. But I knew it took a special kind of patience to cope with her uniqueness. And while Ted was quite possibly the nicest man I'd ever met, the kindest too, he wasn't exactly patient, nor did he tend to hold back what was on his mind. "Don't worry. I'm healing"—which he knew perfectly well, since I'd spent about three hours at the bar ten days or so ago —"wish I wasn't so banged up so I could be there, but shit happens, right?"

He sighed in that melodramatic way he did on occasion. "That it does, sunshine. But you know how I believe in karma, and this isn't about kicking you down."

A rush of air escaped me when I laughed. Ted's regular go-to response to situations was karma. And I liked to think he was right, especially when it meant someone got their comeuppance. I wasn't quite sure how that related to me though. "No? She hasn't got it in for me, huh?"

"Absolutely not. This is one of those 'everything happens for a reason' scenarios, and karma is involved. You're too sweet, my boy, for negativity to be driving her." I didn't get a chance to respond before he continued, asking, "And how is the delectable Billy treating you? Still not dicking you around, right? I can send Jason over—"

"Ha! Not necessary. He's great. Amazing, in fact." Again, I'd already told him this, but that would mean nothing to Ted and whatever he was thinking.

"Hmmm."

"No, no 'hmm.' Whatever you're thinking, I'm not interested. The man is doing me a solid."

"He really is. Why is that exactly?" he asked, just a little too casually, and not for the first time.

I held back my sigh but rolled my eyes. What happened between me and Billy a few months back hadn't been shared with a soul. Well, not on my end, and I couldn't see Billy telling anyone. Holding back was partly because beyond Jason and Ted, there wasn't really anyone to tell. Plus, they'd both taken on this endearing dad-like role with me. It was humbling really. They hadn't known me from Adam when I'd stumbled into their bar asking for work. Truth be told, they still didn't know much more beyond what I'd shared. While I was as genuine as could be, I really didn't want to delve into the pain of my past. Yet despite all of that, they'd supported me, taken me in, given me a job, even arranged the accommodation with Billy.

I owed them a lot. As such, I refused to lie to them outright, fully aware I chose not to disclose everything about me, but in doing so would unearth a whole can of nonsense best left buried where it was.

"Have I lost you?" he asked.

This time I did sigh before saying, "No, I'm here. I've already told you this. Billy's just doing the right thing as my landlord. He knows I can't be by myself at the moment." Though in truth, I was sure with the scooter I had, I could probably manage okay by myself, mostly. "He has a spare room, and last week he didn't really have much work on, so he was looking out for me."

I waited for it, knowing since the Christmas in July do that he'd organized that he was curious about Billy, the man, and also the connection between Billy and me.

"So…," he drew out the word, making me smile, "he would have done the same thing for anyone, right?"

I answered without hesitation, "Yes," believing that to be the truth.

"And it has nothing to do with how the two of you have the hots for each other?"

I closed my eyes and hung my head, defeat pulsing through me. "Ted, I really—"

"No, no, you don't need to confirm or deny, but if he really is such a good guy, which both you and Jasper say he is, then I would have thought now would be the perfect opportunity to explore that chemistry. Because, holy sweet Lord, Lawrence, after just a couple of hours with you in the same room, I nearly pounced on my husbutt from the heat flying off the pair of you. Heck, if just that can turn me on and get me grabbing for Jason's junk, then just imagine what the two of you would be like in the sack."

Of course he had to go there. Silently, I had no other option but to agree with him, knowing full well that even drunk sex with Billy was phenomenal. The thought of getting between the sheets with him again, sober, and the two of us acknowledging the attraction between us…. I shook my head, not sure my heart could take that.

"Oh my good God, you've already done it." He gasped. "I knew it."

"Ted," I said as firmly as possible. When he didn't speak, I expelled a heavy breath, saying, "Please don't."

I heard his breathing down the line, but he remained quiet for a few beats. "Okay, I won't. Just—" He seemed to hesitate a moment before he started again. "Just be safe, and please know both Jason and I are here if you need us, whenever you need us. Any time, day or night," he emphasized. "Okay?"

I smiled despite my pounding heart. "Okay, thanks."

"Perhaps you can come out one night for a few drinks. Ask Billy."

I groaned. "Seriously?"

"What? I only suggested your friendly landlord could get you out of the house one night, is all. That's what friends do, right?"

"Right," I said, defeated.

"But seriously," he continued, "we'd love to see you. It's been too long. We've been worried."

"I know, and thanks, but honestly, I'm okay."

"I'll try to believe you, but it would settle my poor old heart if I could see for myself." I could hear the smile in his voice.

"Well, you are pretty old."

"Hush your mouth, child."

I laughed loudly, relishing the humor that had stopped me focusing on Billy.

"I best go. Husbutt is giving me that brow look that he does. You know the one?"

"I do." I grinned widely, imagining Jason's stern look with dipped brows. It was usually directed at his husband, and usually held the unspoken question of "what now?"

"I hope to see you soon. And promise to call me if you need anything."

"Promise," I said, meaning it. "Thanks, Ted. I'll hopefully see you soon."

"Good. And *be* good," he said just before the line went dead.

I looked at the phone and huffed out an exasperated breath. Exhaustion swept over me. He did have the power to do that at times—wear a person down— though I did recognize it was with good intentions. I yawned loudly, figuring between what I'd achieved so far this morning and that phone call, I deserved a break. My stomach agreeing with a rumble had me making my way to the kitchen and the fridge, knowing there was little in there.

Before the accident, my fridge had been practically bare, with the exception of ketchup, mustard, and a weird jar of pickles I'd won in a raffle last Christmas. I'd been overdue a visit to the supermarket. But the thought of using additional energy to get down the staircase and to Billy's fridge filled me with dread.

I yanked open the door, already with a grimace fixed on my face in expectation. It quickly slipped away to be replaced by surprise. That surprise morphed into another emotion I wasn't quite comfortable with when I found an honest to God square container in there, clearly stuffed with food. Beside it were bottles of water, OJ, and a smoothie.

I removed the plastic container and placed it on the side and clambered onto the stool. Hesitantly, I reached out to open it, aware there was a shake in my hand. But since I was so focused on breathing and trying to ignore the loud beats of my heart, I refused to give my shaking additional attention.

When I opened the clasps of the container, I pressed my lips together.

He'd packed me a proper lunch, complete with a sandwich, fruit, a cookie, and carrot sticks. Balanced on top was a sticky note reading "Eat properly before you take your pills. And stay hydrated."

In the container were also my meds. I swallowed my emotion when I took this all in. Growing up, I'd been privileged to have lunch to take to school every day, courtesy of our housekeeper, Grace. She'd been lovely and kind but was paid to do her job. This, the simple gesture, meant everything.

What the hell was I supposed to do with that?

CHAPTER SEVEN

BILLY

A satisfying pop of bones had me groaning as I stretched my back. With the old shed conversion going strong and almost at completion by Tanner, my focus was building a small, secure yard area attached to what would be a cute two-bedroom home for Frankie and his kid.

Austin and I had worked through plans alongside his brother, Frankie, figuring out how best to accommodate the changes, mainly to make sure it was a safe space for kids while looking homey and being part of the main yard.

Having a break while I'd kept an eye on Lawrence had put me a little behind, but spending the time helping him was more than worth it. Not only had I enjoyed getting to know Lawrence better, despite the circumstances, but it was good to have some downtime too.

Since moving, I'd worked a lot. The distraction had proved so important for my recovery and for settling down. It didn't mean I'd hidden away or didn't think about all that had happened. Instead, keeping busy gave me a new focus.

Lawrence had shifted that.

It had felt good, refreshing to take some time out—yeah, and help Lawrence out too, but it was more than that. For the first time in years, I'd had quiet time to myself, mainly when Lawrence was napping in the first few days of strong drugs that made him drowsy. And during those moments, I didn't shy away from the lack of distraction. I didn't chase a task to keep me busy.

I swiped my forearm over my sweaty brow and smiled at the thought.

"All good out here?"

I turned to look at Frankie, offering him a smile, my gaze moving to his boy, Tyler, who stood with a frisbee clasped in his hands.

"Yeah, the heat's a bit of a killer, but I think I've made decent progress today," I answered before returning my attention to Tyler. "You looking for Penny, buddy?"

The kid nodded and smiled shyly. This boy had been through hell and back since his mom's passing, but his smiles were coming a little easier.

"She's just inside the house. Why don't you go and open the door for her? I'm sure she'd love to play."

Tyler's bright blue eyes lit up, and he glanced up at his dad.

"Sure you can. Just mind your fingers on the door," Frankie answered, reaching down and ruffling his hair, softness in his eyes.

Tyler sped away, Frankie's focus following his progress.

"How's he doing?" I asked, aware Frankie started work next week so had been easing his kid into childcare.

A small shrug was his initial response before he turned his attention to me. "He'll be okay. He's had three sessions there now and came back happy enough. Was clingy as hell to start with." I ignored the large swallow he took and simply stood with a smile, waiting for him to finish. "I've been reading books about grief and shit, you know?"

I nodded, thinking back to the books my counselor had insisted I check out some time back.

"Through all the drivel, I managed to pull out some helpful pointers, I think. Making it clear that I'll be there for him, made sure he also knows he has his uncles Austin and Jasper too, and making sure my ass is never late for him."

"Looks like you'll both be fine. It's good you've eased him into it and starting a new routine, right?" Georgia had told me that a time or two.

"I know. Feel like shit leaving him though. Never knew it could feel like this." He rubbed at his chest, looking in the direction of the house.

"What's that?"

"The pain with loving someone so much."

I gave him a soft smile. "I've heard about it on more than a few occasions, especially with kids."

The noise of a door slamming, a bark, and a loud, childish giggle filtered through the air, making both of us smile. Penny came into view first, her tongue hanging out as she raced away before backtracking. Tyler appeared next, charging behind her, calling her name.

"I can't remember a time before he came into my life." His words were awed, soft, and while I didn't have that sort of connection, and couldn't ever imagine having it either, I liked to think I understood.

"He's a resilient kid," I said.

"He is." Frankie nodded, his smile soft and much lighter than it had been. His gaze then traveled around me. "You need a hand with anything while Tyler's being entertained by Penny?"

"Absolutely," I said. "These frames are a two-man job, so that'd be great."

We worked together in companionable silence, straining a little at the post we lifted, which would form the lintel to the playhouse I was building. With Tyler's laughter and Penny's happy barks as the soundtrack to my afternoon, it was easy to get lost in the fantasy of the idea of family.

Having a child had never been in my plan. And even though Tyler was a good kid, so I knew they existed, my mind hadn't changed. But a dog would be kinda nice one day. Though I'd always imagined a couple of dogs would come after I'd settled. It didn't matter that there hadn't been anyone in a helluva long time. The dream of finding someone and falling for them was still present. Perhaps it had been tucked away for a while, buried in my own grief and loss. But it wasn't lost completely.

And then there was Lawrence.

He was the first man in a long time to have caught

my attention, to the point where I wondered if he were a dog person or not. Last month I'd watched him play with a cute puppy that his bosses had. He'd seemed happy enough, content with the bundle of fluff licking all over him.

It was when he'd been on the floor playing with Biscuit—I didn't spend too much time wondering why Ted and Jason would call their dog after food—that my heart had flipped over itself a time or two, the first in a long time. And all because of his loud, carefree laugh. On hearing it, I'd been left wide-eyed and filled with guilt. He'd gifted me that same laugh a time or two before I'd screwed it all up.

And now I wanted more.

I wanted all of his laughs, all of his content sighs, and that was just from the luxury of this extra time we'd spent together.

I had my work cut out for me to make things right, to get him to trust me. But Lawrence was worth it. The knowledge wrapped around me, certainty in its caress.

"Shit, what time is it?" I asked, tugging my phone out of my back pocket. It was just after two thirty, and I hadn't called Lawrence to make sure he was okay.

"Something wrong?" Frankie asked, concern evident in his tone.

"I haven't checked on Lawrence today to make sure he's all right."

"Ahh." Amusement filled that one sound, drawing my eyes in Frankie's direction.

"Ahh, what?"

He grinned. "How are the living arrangements going?"

My brows dipped low, wondering where he was going with this. "All good. He's managing better, becoming more mobile."

"Uh-huh."

"Uh-huh, what?" I peered down at my phone, double-checking I didn't have any missed calls from Lawrence before returning my focus to Frankie.

He shrugged, wearing a smirk. "Just wondering if you two were hooking up, is all."

I snorted. "Hell, just come right out and say it, man."

His grin stretched. "Beating around the bush is time-consuming. Easier to just ask. So, are you?"

I rolled my eyes and shook my head. "You all been gossiping about this?"

"If by 'you all' you mean Jasper and Austin, then more Jasper than my brother. But I know that a couple of his friends who know Lawrence have been talking about it too."

"Jesus. You got nothing better to do with your time?" There was no sharpness in my tone, but it didn't mean I wanted to be the source of gossip.

"Nah, not really. Maybe next week when I'm working. So, are you?"

I huffed out a breath and pulled up Lawrence's name, ready to hit Call. "Nope, we're not. Feel free to report back."

Frankie laughed. "I absolutely will."

"You do that," I said, stepping away to make the call with some semblance of privacy.

After the sixth ring, Lawrence's voice mail kicked in. I looked at the screen and frowned, not quite sure what I was looking for exactly, but not liking that he hadn't picked up. It was likely his phone was not in the same room, so not getting to the phone in time wasn't a surprise. But not knowing he was okay and hadn't hurt himself in some way had a ball forming in the pit of my gut.

I tried again and stretched my neck from side to side. After spending years as a cop, there were several aspects of my personality that I'd honed—listening to my gut, keeping calm under pressure, and not reacting emotionally.

But since the accident, two of those three had all

but disintegrated. And the first, well, I didn't know whether I had faith in that anymore either.

Once again, there was no answer.

"You okay?" Frankie's voice startled me, pulling me away from focusing on the edge of panic worming its way into my system.

"Yeah." I glanced in his direction and noted the worry in his eyes. "He's just not answering. I'm sure he's fine," I said, trying to convince myself more than him. I tried to cut off the direction of my thoughts as they reminded me Lawrence said he planned to do some decorating. Those damn steps were a nightmare for him. He could have fallen, could be injured—

"I'm sure he is, but if you're worried, why don't you head on home?"

I nodded. "Yeah. Think I will. I was going to take Penny—"

"All good," Frankie said, interrupting me. "Tyler and I will look after her. Take her to the dog park or something."

"Yeah, that'd be great, thanks."

"No problem. I'll even pack up here for you."

I smiled in relief. "I owe you one. Seriously, thank you."

He shooed me away before seeking out his boy still

playing with Penny. "Just let me know if something's wrong, okay?"

I backed away toward my car. "Will do." I threw him a tight smile and dug out my keys from the glove box.

Once the engine was running, I took a few deep breaths. My overreaction was exactly that, but with tomorrow being the shittiest day of the year, my nerves were already fried. My concern for Lawrence, my developing feelings for the man combined with the time of year meant my thinking wasn't exactly clear.

After a deep inhale, I pulled out of Austin's driveway, forcing myself to calm down and not think the worst.

I GLANCED OVER THE HALF-PAINTED WALLS, THE SPILLED paint, and the mishmash of splotches and footprints. A few steps past the disturbance, and I finally felt able to take a deep breath, one that actually cleared my head.

Lawrence lay asleep on the bare mattress on the floor, a dust sheet tucked under his head, the same paint evident on the discarded shirt to the side of him. Smears of blue dotted his neck, his forearms, and his face. His exposed side and what I could see of his upper body were paint-free. His chest moved steadily as his eyes remained shut, and I didn't think I'd ever been more pleased to see someone sleep on the job.

I'd already spotted his phone in the kitchen, had taken a look, seen my missed calls, and also noted it was on silent. That was something I'd be having words with Lawrence about, all too aware that while recovering he was vulnerable. There was no doubt my need for him to have his cell ring out was completely for my benefit and was my issue, but for my own sanity, I needed to be able to ensure he was okay. Safe.

I eased out of the room, my heart finally giving up its erratic beat and slowing to a steady strum. It was clear some sort of mishap had occurred, but the important thing was he was unharmed, or so I assumed from his sleeping form.

As my muscles relaxed, tension lessening in my body, I started work on cleaning up the spilled paint as best as I could. From the spoiled paper crammed into a garbage bag, it looked like Lawrence had attempted to mop up the spillage, but somewhere along the way, he'd given up. I imagined exhaustion had tugged him to the mattress.

It didn't take long to clean up the area. I'd just gathered the couple of trash bags, heading toward the door, when the sound of movement and a soft groan caught my attention. I dropped the bags next to the front door and made my way to the bedroom. Awake and sitting up, Lawrence brushed a hand over his head. His arm muscles bunched and moved, drawing my attention to them.

That one night when we'd stayed together, I hadn't truly appreciated Lawrence's body, let alone the man himself. Too drunk and absorbed in my own feelings, I hadn't given him the time or attention he deserved.

What I wouldn't give to change that situation.

"Hey," I said, my voice gruff, lower than I anticipated. The sound startled a reaction out of him as he dropped his hand immediately and whipped his head in my direction.

"Holy hell, you scared me." His good arm moved, his hand settling over his naked chest above his heart. "Jesus."

Amusement licked at me, and I smiled despite my earlier frustration. "Sorry. 'Hey' is pretty much a warning cue though."

He shot me a look that was all sass, and I could only imagine the sarcastic comeback bouncing around in his head.

"You hurt yourself in whatever happened out there?" I indicated behind me and watched embarrassment cross over his features.

"Urgh. I tried to clean up—"

"It's all good. It's done. It didn't take long. I'm more concerned in knowing if you hurt yourself."

He'd tugged his lower lip into his mouth as I spoke, gnawing at the damn thing, pulling my attention away from where it should be: on his health rather than wondering if I'd ever have the opportunity to kiss him again.

"I'm okay."

I narrowed my eyes. "That's not what I was asking. Did you hurt yourself?"

He released his lip and huffed out a breath. I held back my amusement, aware he'd figured I wouldn't allow bullshit. "I jolted my arm when I fell."

I straightened up in the doorway and stepped further into the room before crouching down at the end of the mattress.

"You fell?"

"Yes, I was a dick. Don't ask."

I pressed my lips together, struggling with that request. Truth was, it didn't really matter how it happened as long as he was okay. "Okay, so you hit it, fall on it? Do we need to head out and get you another scan?"

Lawrence's head moved from left to right before I'd finished speaking. "Nope, and neither. I managed to catch myself with my good arm, but my wrist didn't like the whole-body shudder that came with it. Took me a beat to get my breath back is all. I took some of those stronger painkillers, the ones that make me tired, and dragged my ass here midway through clearing up."

Reading people had once upon a time been my forte. As Lawrence spoke, I zeroed in on him, looking for any signs he wasn't being truthful. The last thing I wanted was for him to damage any of his healing bones. Satisfied he told the truth, I smiled. "You ready to head to the house, get cleaned up yourself?"

His eyes shot wide at that, a blush spreading across his cheeks when he glanced down at himself. He snorted. "I'm a bit of a wreck, huh?"

I laughed. "Nothing a hose down won't cure."

His gaze connected with mine and a smile curved his mouth. "As long as it doesn't involve you turning a water pipe on me, that sounds good."

Reaching out my hand for him as I stood, I waited for him to grip my palm. He did so immediately, and I helped him stand, belatedly looking around, remembering I'd seen his scooter at the bottom of the staircase outside.

Toe-to-toe, I placed a hand on his waist, keeping him steady and trying not to inhale his scent too deeply. Being so close, it would be easy to lean in, capture his mouth, but with all that had happened, taking what I wanted when he was vulnerable wasn't how I would play this.

Unable to look away from his piercing gaze, I took the moment to absorb the closeness, knowing doing so was as risky as inhaling his masculine scent. His skin was warm under my palm, soft above the ridges of his muscles. I'd had many moments of regret in my life, and pushing away this man, the same guy whose steel-gray eyes seemed almost storm-like as they connected to mine as we stood so close, was one that hurt.

Without pulling away, I asked, "You okay putting some weight on your boot or you need me to help you?"

His lips parted before a slight uptick of the side of his mouth followed. "You've got a thing with me being in your arms, huh?"

"It's something I could get used to," I said without preamble and meaning every word.

His eyes widened a fraction, the only tell as he said, "I can manage on my boot, but you being a crutch just in case would be great, thanks."

Not missing a beat, I responded, "You've got a thing with wanting me close, huh?"

A smile so damn perfect appeared on his mouth. "It's something I could get used to," he shot back, his voice light and teasing. My grin immediately followed as I led him through the small apartment and back to my house.

CHAPTER EIGHT

Living in a state of being permanently hot and bothered was my new norm.

This Billy, the one who was kind and caring and witty, was so much more than the sweet guy I'd begun to become tentative friends with all those months ago. He seemed more open, certainly more obvious with what I read very clearly was attraction for me. And while that knowledge was heady for my ego, it freakin' terrified me.

I'd shut away thoughts of him when he'd screwed me over, literally. But Billy was proving to be a difficult man to ignore.

"I forgot to say thanks for packing my lunch for me earlier." I worked hard at controlling my voice, not wanting to give away just how sweet that gesture had been.

Billy looked up from the grill. We were eating outside again, something we tended to do at least a couple of times a week. It was nice being outside to cook and eat. Growing up, I'd never really had the chance for a cookout unless it was a forced display with my mother's political friends. It certainly hadn't been simply throwing meat on the grill and kicking back with laughter and chilled conversation, which I'd enviously watched on TV shows.

"It's all good. No big deal."

His response was casual, and perhaps I should have left it at that, but him looking out for me that way *was* a big deal for me. "I appreciate it. No one's ever done anything like that for me before."

When his gaze connected with mine, I looked away, not quite sure if I wished I could take those words back or not. Opening up wouldn't do anything other than drag up bitterness and hurt.

After a beat of silence, he said, "In that case, I'm glad I did." His gaze held mine before returning to the steaks, and a small smile curved my lips, happy he didn't push or question. As a former cop, it must have taken a bucketload of control to not fire away with questions to pry deeper. Instead, he'd given me grace and not pushed.

"How are you getting on with the play area you're building?"

Not skipping a beat despite my change in subject, Billy grinned and looked my way. "Yeah, good. It's all coming together. Frankie gave me a hand today while his kid exhausted Penny."

I laughed, sure Penny had loved that. "That's great. Frankie seems like a nice guy." I didn't know the man all that well, but from what I'd heard, he'd survived a life-threatening accident, had his own healing to navigate, and had only recently discovered he was a dad.

"Yeah, seems like a good guy. Handling his new lot okay too. Starts a job next week."

"That's great."

"Yeah, finding routine and all that's good for kids, right?"

I smiled at the uncertainty in Billy's voice. "Yeah, so I've heard. You been around kids much?" I asked, curious about anything to do with Billy. While I knew some aspects of his family, there was still a lot left to learn.

"A bit," he said, placing the steaks on a plate, then coming over to the table where I sat. "I told you about my nieces and nephews, but I don't see them as much as I should. I spent a good amount of time with my partner's kids." He slammed his mouth shut at that, eyes peering off into the distance. I could all but see him shutting down before me.

The need to know more and hear him talk rode me hard, but I wouldn't push, especially after he'd showed me the same courtesy a while ago.

"I've never been around kids other than my sister," I said, sticking with the topic but pulling the focus back onto me as best as I could. "I have a kid sister." I smiled, thinking about Mary. "Well, she's not so much a kid anymore." While our contact was limited, we managed to touch base a handful of times a year, so I sort of felt like I knew what was going on in her life. The latest being that she was engaged.

The thought horrified me, as she was so damn young, and I was scared it was a relationship pushed by our mom. But getting married would mean she'd be out from under our mother's tight control, so there was that.

My shoulders relaxed when Billy glanced at me, the faraway look in his eyes no longer visible. Instead, interest shone in their depths. I hadn't discussed Mary with anyone in a long time.

"How much younger is she?"

I eased into this topic, despite the red flags

surrounding anything else family related. "Six years. She's just turned twenty-one." The familiar pang hit my chest. It was one more year I hadn't celebrated with her. But I'd sent her a card, signed with the usual *Happy birthday, buttercup. Love, Laurie.* I had no doubt mail was screened to some extent, and Laurie had always been her go-to name for me growing up, with my name being impossible for her to say until she was five.

Every year I was surprised when she thanked me for my card, having expected Mom to throw it away to try to sever all connection.

"Wow, twenty-one, huh. Those were the days." A smile curled his lips, and I laughed.

"Hell, you're not that old." I wasn't exactly sure how old Billy was. Yeah, he was older than me, perhaps by ten years. I'd never thought to ask. Not because of my lack of interest in the man, but because his age didn't impact on how hot he was or how much I liked him.

He quirked his brow at me, pausing from cutting into his steak. "Did you just put emphasis on *that*?"

I snorted. "Nope. Your age doesn't factor into the man you are," I said honestly.

His head tilt and eye contact had me pausing. Then I gaped when he said, "So no daddy kink I should know about?" My mouth was still open when he laughed hard. "Holy shit, your face." He continued to laugh, his eyes filling with tears.

Reacting, I picked up a cherry tomato from my plate and threw it at him, joining in with his laughter when it bounced off his forehead. "Daddy kink would imply you're a man with a certain amount of maturity," I said around my laugh. "That's clearly not the case."

His laughter slowed. "True." He followed up with a wink, a smile still curling his lips.

Our meal continued with talking and smiles, the latter coming readily despite the more somber moments earlier. Billy was easy to talk to, amazing, really, considering all our months of awkward small talk and polite conversation. By the time I yawned, tiredness biting at my heels, I grinned inwardly, wondering at the turn of events and how a stupid accident resulted in the destruction of the barriers we'd put in place.

The warmth spreading through me wasn't even from the two beers I'd had—low alcohol, courtesy of Billy and his worry about my painkillers. Between our growing familiarity, my comfort with him, as well as enjoying the friendships I'd made at work, for the first time ever, contentment made a tentative path through me. Nervous and most definitely hesitant, the sense of comfort was there nonetheless. The unfamiliar sensation perhaps should have set me on edge, but right then, as I yawned, drawing a gentle look from Billy, I embraced the newness with everything I had.

Billy's hand on my shoulder startled me, pulling me away from my thoughts. "Time for bed," he said, tenderness in his voice that I liked a little too much.

I nodded, my gaze landing on the empty bowls and beer bottles. "Let me just help clear up."

"I've got it. You've had a busy day, plus there was the fall."

I gave him a sleepy smile. "I'm fine."

"I know, but you need rest."

There was no point debating this with him. Billy's stubbornness knew no bounds. "Okay. Thanks."

Billy bobbed his head. "I'll help you inside, but call if you need anything."

No longer were his touches tentative. After the accident, there'd been no time for that. I loved the sure grip he had on me, the immediate heat that followed on contact. While I could easily manage the few steps needed around his house, I shamelessly leaned into his supportive hold, lapping up his closeness and attention and wishing it wouldn't end so soon.

At the bathroom, we stopped, my gaze traveling to

his. His focus was already on me, an intensity there I hadn't seen before. Not even all those months ago.

He hesitated when his mouth parted, as though not sure whether or not to speak. When he pressed his lips together, I thought he'd made his decision. I offered a small smile and a thanks, preparing to enter the bathroom, my hand already on the handle when his words had me pausing.

"Listen, I should warn you, tomorrow's going to be a shit day for me."

I frowned and looked back at him, not liking the uncertainty and the vulnerability in his voice. His eyes searched mine a moment. I nodded, not wanting to stop his words since whatever he was saying was clearly a struggle.

"I just…." The tremble had him trailing off. Instinctively, I reached out, my palm to his forearm, and gave a gentle squeeze. "It's the anniversary of Clark's death." He swallowed. "When I was a cop, he was my partner."

Sorrow clouded his features and all but ripped my heart out. Pain rolled off him in waves. I'd had no idea the man before me had been hurting so much. It was scary how well we as humans could conceal the sadness that often gripped our hearts. I'd perfected it over the years, but Billy's raw pain left me catching my breath.

I didn't know how to respond, how to act. Did he want a hug, want words of understanding that I couldn't really give? My own loss was so different. Platitudes wouldn't be right.

Billy pulled his gaze away, focusing on my hand on his arm and the thumb strokes I brushed over his skin. With his eyes downcast and his distress no longer beating at me through the eye contact, I offered, "I'm here, and I can be here for you, or not. Whatever you need."

He flicked his head up, his gaze reconnecting with mine, and I'd never been so relieved to see the small, if not tentative, smile on his lips. "Thanks. A drinking buddy may be nice."

My own lips curved at that, as I already mentally planned to make sure I didn't take any pain meds tomorrow. "That I can do. Perhaps we can order takeout?"

"Yeah." He nodded. "That'd be good." He stepped back and my hand fell away. "Night, Lawrence. Call out if you need anything."

I bobbed my head. "Will do. Sleep well." Hand back on the handle, I opened the door and stepped away, shutting it and leaning back against the door. Closing my eyes, I wondered what had happened to his partner, how he'd died, and I couldn't help but wonder if that was the reason why he'd retired from the police force so early.

Early morning sunshine filtered into Billy's spare room, where I'd taken up residence over the past few weeks. Light and shadows danced across the wall from the swaying trees outside, the movement hypnotic and relaxing.

It took me a while to fall asleep the previous night, my brain working overtime thinking about Billy, his loss, and what today would bring. He'd previously told me he had today off, and while I had no idea of his plans, I'd thought of a few possibilities of how we could spend the day—if he wanted to spend it with me, that was.

I'd psyched myself up to sharing my ideas, just like I'd prepared myself for him saying no. Either way would be fine. Today was not about me or my needs or feelings. As such, I'd do whatever I could to support Billy on the anniversary of his friend's death.

Escapism or reflection, I mused as I got my ass out of bed, were a possibility, and both were on offer. I washed up and dressed, then headed to the kitchen where I could already hear Billy moving around, cooking pancakes, from the scent drifting in the air.

I rounded the corner and took in the scene before me. A pretty sight greeted me with a shirtless Billy, barefooted, and with jeans molding his backside perfectly. It was difficult to get words out coherently at the best of times, but with Billy like this, I didn't think I'd be able to speak without becoming tongue-tied.

I chewed my lip, unable to pull my gaze away from his exposed skin. There were a few scars marring his right side, which I hadn't noticed before. Rather than being ugly, they seemed as much a part of the man's beauty as the unblemished areas.

There was no doubt I appreciated his body, but Billy was so much more than a handsome man with skin I'd happily lick. And these scars, much like the man, told me there was a depth to Billy I'd only just started to uncover.

"Hey."

His warm voice had me starting and dragging my gaze to his face. With his back still toward me, he'd angled his head to peer behind him. His smile was soft, eyes confidently holding mine.

"Pancakes are almost done."

"They smell great," I said, hobbling further into the

room. I glanced around, noting plates were out but no utensils. I headed to the drawer and pulled out knives and forks, taking them to the table off to the right of the kitchen.

Billy watched my movements a moment before returning his attention to flipping the pancake, managing a high flip that made me laugh.

While I couldn't see his face as I went in search of the syrup and butter, Billy's smile was obvious when he said, "Clark flipped a pretty mean pancake."

I fought hard not to pause, not wanting to draw attention to him sharing stories with me. But hell if his words didn't send warmth racing through me.

"He used to organize this crazy pancake day, something his parents brought him up with. They moved from England before he was born." Billy's laugh was gentle as he plated the pancakes and turned toward me, indicating for me to sit. "He used to make these shitty pancakes that were super thin and put sugar and lemon on them, force everyone at the station to eat them and celebrate what he called Shrove Tuesday." The shake of his head followed his words, his eyes alive with humor. "I used to threaten to use them as an interrogation technique."

He snorted as he sat and placed down the

mounded plate. I glanced at them, relieved they were proper fluffy pancakes.

"Don't worry. I like you too much to punish you with Clark's pancakes." A wink accompanied his words, and I grinned, equally surprised and happy this was how Billy was handling today.

"I've never been more pleased to hear you like me," I jested, picking up the butter to spread on my breakfast. "If you ever pull thin pancakes out and offer them up to me, I know I'm in trouble." I grinned before I ate a forkful of pancake. Sugary sweetness combined perfectly with the savory pancake. "Damn," I said, talking around a mouthful, "these are seriously good." An enthusiastic nod followed another mouthful.

Billy looked pleased with himself as he placed our coffee down and sat, starting to dig in. "Yeah. I won the pancake cook-off four years in a row back at my old station." A happy smirk pulled at his lips. It suited him, and I hoped I'd get to see that smile regularly.

"Impressive," I said before taking a sip of hot coffee. "And I can see why. Tasty as hell, man."

Billy's smirk stretched even wider before he put a forkful of pancake smothered in syrup in his mouth.

After a few more mouthfuls, I ventured into sharing my ideas for the day. "I'm not sure how you want to spend your day, but I've a couple of ideas if you want to hear them."

Billy quirked his brow at me. "Other than some drinks tonight, nothing. So go for it." Intrigue colored his words, and I thought I heard a gentleness to them too. I needed him to know I cared and wanted him to get through this day as best as he could. And from his open conversation about Clark, I was hopeful he'd be open to my ideas.

I took another sip of coffee before clearing my throat and fortifying my nerves. "They're playing a special anniversary screening of *Beverly Hills Cop* over in Fairbanks this afternoon. I thought it would be fun to go watch that. On the way we could grab lunch, maybe in Pickton, then after the movie, we could stop at that brewery, Beechams, do a couple of samples, maybe grab a snack before heading back. If not, then we—"

"You had me at *Beverly Hills Cop*," he said with a laugh, interrupting me. "That all sounds really great."

I didn't disguise my pleasure when I asked, "Yeah?"

"Yeah, definitely. Sounds like a date." The wink that followed that simple announcement made my stomach flip over itself. The day being an honest-to-God date was not what I'd intended, but there was no way I'd be allowing take-backs. I inwardly snorted, wondering if there'd been a single moment or if it was the combination of a bunch of them that had me changing my tune about Billy.

Was it only a few weeks ago I'd been so determined not to let this man in again?

His words pulled me from my musings when he said, "On the way, we can stop in at the bar where you work if you want? Figured you'd like to say hello, since it's been a couple of weeks."

"Really?" My heart stumbled at his thoughtfulness.

"Definitely. We won't stay for long if we want to make good on your plans, but I'm sure you've been missing out on seeing familiar faces."

"I don't mind your face so much." The words flew out on their own accord, but I didn't have time to be embarrassed, not with the goofy smile that lit up Billy's features.

"I don't mind your face either." That wink of his once again followed. Before now, I hadn't thought winking had the power to gain a reaction from me other than an eye roll, but Billy's winks hit their mark time and time again. "Let's finish up, then we can get some fresh air before heading to Kirkby," he said as he picked up his coffee mug.

I grinned in response, already liking the direction this day was taking.

CHAPTER NINE

BILLY

THE BAR SOMEHOW MANAGED TO LOOK FRESH AND modern yet complete with small-town charm. It was something that always struck me whenever I came here. With the bar not yet open this morning, the quiet was refreshing rather than feeling strange in the usually loud place. We sat outside in the bar's yard, the same place where we'd celebrated in July. That already seemed such a long time ago, despite it only being early September.

Sitting on the surprisingly comfortable bench seat, I nursed the small cup of coffee. It was a little strong for easy drinking, so tentative sips it was.

"Ooh, I heard about that. They're doing a whole *Beverly Hills Cop* marathon, right?" Ted said, eyes alight and bouncing between Lawrence and me. I had no doubt he was looking for tells, trying to see what he could read into the two of us being together, our potential relationship. Subtlety was not Ted's strength.

"Yeah," Lawrence responded, "we're just going to watch the first. I know it's a pretty old film—"

Jason laughed while Ted and I scoffed simultaneously. "It's not that old," I said, immediately recalling the similar words I'd spoken yesterday.

Lawrence didn't even try to hide his smile. He cast me a quick look before focusing on Jason, Ted's husband, who was just a few years older than Lawrence. "Anything before we were born is a classic, right, Jase?"

He laughed. "Don't get me involved in this." He paused the barest of moments before tagging on, "But yeah, it's a classic."

Laughter followed, Lawrence's immediately distinguishable and increasingly familiar. I liked the sound a lot. I especially liked the way his cheeks crinkled up and the way his eyes captured his joy.

"Millennials," Ted chastised with zero heat. "There's absolutely no hope for the future."

I grinned as both Jason and Lawrence rolled their eyes.

"So, not the whole marathon?" Ted then said, bringing the conversation back on track.

"I thought just the one?" Lawrence said, looking directly at me, his voice pitching into a question.

"One's good for me." When Lawrence had made the offer to spend the day with me, I'd been happy, but when he'd gone one step further and offered specific plans, letting me know he'd thought carefully about today, I'd been touched.

Not only had he clearly spent last night thinking about me, but he wanted to spend the day too, knowing its significance.

Every year had been a struggle. But this year was the first time I had managed genuine laughter and smiles. It was the first time I'd thought about Clark's life rather than only his death.

It was cathartic, and without Lawrence, none of that would have been possible.

"And how are you healing?" Jason asked, focusing on Lawrence.

"Good. I'm using my hand more—"

"I just bet you are, my sweet melon dew," Ted said, cutting Lawrence off.

"—and managing on my boot," Lawrence continued without missing a beat, shaking his head at Ted as he spoke, "as long as I don't push it too much." My lips twitched as Lawrence simply went on as though Ted wasn't baiting him. "I have X-rays next week to check on how they're healing." Lawrence glanced in my direction before focusing back on Jason. "I don't suppose one of you can take me to the appointment. It's early so shouldn't impact—"

"I've already planned to take you," I said, interrupting him and drawing all three gazes to me. I kept my focus on Lawrence. "Next Wednesday at eight thirty."

Pink whispered across Lawrence's skin, and his lips curved high. "That okay? You don't mind?"

"Of course. I said I'd take care of you. I meant it."

Out of the corner of my eye, I didn't miss Ted reaching out and gripping his husband's arm, but I was determined to keep focused on Lawrence, whose happiness was so easy to read.

"Thanks, Billy," he said, his tone gentle, affectionate.

"You keep that blissed-out smile on Lawrence's gorgeous face, Billy dear, and you will have coffee on the house anytime you're here."

Still making eye contact with Lawrence, I watched, mesmerized, as his blush deepened, not quite caring about Ted's words or his offer of too-strong coffee. Instead, I latched on to how Ted, who I figured knew Lawrence the most, recognized the impact I was having on Lawrence, and absolutely for the better.

The knowledge kick-started my heart into double time. I hadn't attempted to deny how much I liked Lawrence and wanted more than friendship. How could I when he gave me a calm and peace unlike any other? Yeah, that was in complete juxtaposition of the fast-paced heartbeat and somersaults in my stomach, but along with my affection was a blissful stillness, almost contentment.

I'd be a fool to not chase that feeling.

With the silence continuing perhaps too long, I found my voice, saying, "How about I keep that smile just for me? I think that's reward enough."

The loud sigh from Ted made me smile, but the silent exchange between me and Lawrence, filled with possibility, settled something inside me soul deep.

THE FOURTH SHOT OF WHISKEY WENT DOWN MUCH smoother. Yet I still chased it with a gulp of my cold beer. Whiskey was not my friend, and I totally knew better. The last time I'd indulged, I'd been with Clark and had ended up having to be carried out of the bar before I humiliated myself with a striptease.

To be fair, I'd been a rookie, but I still should have known better.

That night many years ago had ended up with me propped up in his bathroom, clinging onto the toilet bowl for dear life. Not my finest hour, but Clark had enjoyed the night so much that he'd reminded me of it regularly.

Tonight I hoped like hell I wouldn't be in the same situation, but it kinda felt right to be doing so now, taking shots on the anniversary of Clark's death. As soon as we were back home after one of the best days I could remember having, the glass and bottle were in my hand. And when Lawrence had appeared in the doorway after taking a quick shower, soft concern etched on his face, it had been a no-brainer to pour him a glass and grab him a beer too.

While I was on my way to being wasted, it didn't deter from my smiles when I shared with Lawrence some stories about Clark. "Shit, and when he met Candy, a woman who he'd helped rescue from a mugging one night—" I snorted before throwing back another shot. I didn't even wince this time. Not at the burn. Not at the taste. That right there should have told me to stop. But still, I grinned, continuing, "—she went all *Fatal Attraction* on his ass, broke into his apartment and shit."

"Jesus, that sounds terrifying." Lawrence's eyes

were wide, and through my squint, it was obvious he was nowhere near as hammered as I was.

"Had to get a restraining order on her." I shook my head in memory. Clark had been mortified, Georgia had been pissed, but years after, we'd laughed our asses off at the situation." Refusing to dwell on the fact there'd never be new memories, I added, "Everyone at the station gave him hell, but he handled it."

Lawrence tilted his head. "He sounds like he was a really great guy."

I pushed aside the ache in my chest. "He was the best man I've ever known." I cleared my throat and glanced away, not willing to lose myself to emotion. My day with Lawrence really had been incredible, and I didn't want the sweetness of the day to be lost in despair, but memories of Clark were too close to the surface for me to shut them down.

As if sensing I was on edge, Lawrence pushed the subject in another direction. "I'm sure he had a ton of stories to tell about you too."

I grinned, turning my attention back to the man who I'd decided to spill all of this on tonight. After four weeks or so of living in each other's space, there was no doubt we were friends. And after today, I thought we were close to being something more. There was this hard-on-inducing chemistry between us for one, but I trusted Lawrence, enjoyed his company, his sweetness and humor.

I turned a little on the couch, angling toward him more fully. We'd gravitated to the sitting area a couple of drinks back, our empty bottles and whiskey on the wooden table an arm's length away. "He could have told you some stories I know I'd rather forget." I shook my head, surprising myself that happiness chased my words. "When Georgia finally gets her ass into gear and pays us a visit, you'll have to ask her yourself. There was nothing she didn't know about Clark. He couldn't keep anything from her."

"Georgia?" Lawrence's brows dipped. "Was that his wife?"

"Yeah. They were married before we met. Were actually high school sweethearts." I chuckled. "I complained regularly about missing out on his bachelor party and wedding." I seriously had. I was such a pain in their asses. My complaints paid off though. "For their tenth wedding anniversary, I talked them into renewing their vows in Vegas."

Lawrence chuckled. "Really? They fell for it?"

"Yeah, Georgia loved me. I could sweet-talk her into pretty much anything. Made it my mission just to piss Clark off."

"Geez, remind me never to get on your bad side."

He scrunched his nose. "Between the possibility of soggy pancakes and whatever else you could throw at me…." He trailed off, shaking his head, his smirk negating his move.

I grinned wide and shook my head too. "You've got it all wrong. It's when I love you that you have to worry."

Eyes wide, lips parting, Lawrence caught his breath. It was loud in the silence that had followed my words. I simply stared at him, not quite sure how to follow up my statement. The truth was, beyond all those months ago when I'd had the hottest night of my life with the man before me, I'd never been in love. While I loved my friends and family hard and fierce, the love of a man with hearts and rainbows and uncovered cocks had never happened.

And then there was Lawrence with his sweet and fun temperament. I enjoyed spending my time with him a helluva lot. The thought of love someday with the guy? I internally shrugged. I would not be running for the hills if that happened.

After taking a big gulp of beer, Lawrence said, "And is she planning on visiting soon?"

I sighed, admitting, "Maybe, hopefully. She kinda banned me from seeing her and interfering in any aspect of her life a while ago." My words were coming out fast and thick, and I figured now, with the shove of booze behind me, was about as good a time as ever. "It was just before I was a prick to you."

"Oh, wow, okay." His gaze remained fixed on mine.

"Yeah. After Clark died, and while recovering from my injuries—"

"You were injured?"

I waved him off. "Another time."

He pursed his lips but nodded, indicating for me to go on.

"So yeah, I was a mess, but I was also a little overbearing, protective of Georgia and her boys." Lawrence's frown had me explaining, "I put a ridiculous security system in her house, investigated her neighbors even when not active on the force, and threatened a couple of her male colleagues who were sniffing around."

"Okay." He dragged out the word, a combination of amusement and uncertainty in his response.

"So I became a little full-on protecting Georgia and the boys, needing to look out for them and make sure they were safe. The doc said I was suffering from PTSD." I shrugged, my intention not to belittle the situation or my diagnosis, but simply acknowledging the truth of that time in my life. "So eventually, in a combination of being pissed off with me but also wanting to move closer to her parents, she and the boys moved to Florida. And I came here. A complete break."

Lawrence placed his empty bottle on the table and passed me a water. I chuckled a little, having no idea when he'd grabbed the drink, but recognizing he was right. I was already sobering a fraction from the real talk, and water wasn't a bad idea.

"So what happened a few months back?" Interest was ablaze in his eyes, and not for the first time, guilt slithered through me. We could have been doing this —hanging out, being friends—and had something real for eight months. Disappointment settled in my chest at the thought. I heaved out a breath, trying to shake my shitty actions away. Living in regret was unhealthy. My counselor had drilled that into me virtually every session.

"Georgia contacted me, letting me know she'd started dating." Shame was an ugly fucking emotion.

"Shit, okay." He nodded, no doubt putting every-thing together. "That night you'd drank a lot, you know when…?" he said, trailing off. He cleared his throat. "Was that the night you found out, when she told you?"

I closed my eyes and nodded. "Yeah." I forced my lids open and made eye contact. He deserved to see how truly sorry I was. "It was a rough day. I overreacted, seriously pissed her off, may have threatened to head on over to Florida that night." I winced. "Yeah, I had some shit to sort out."

"And you have?"

I watched the slow movement of his chest, my gaze drifting to his Adam's apple, enjoying how it bobbed when he swallowed, before I met his eyes. "I have. I had a few sessions with a local counselor. She helped me through it. Delved back into my PTSD and had me recognize that while I was going through the motions and seeming to be living my life happily, I was full of shit."

I wanted to look away. Needed to disconnect as tears sprang in my eyes. But I couldn't. Caught up in Lawrence's kind gaze, I also needed, wanted, absolutely fucking had to let him see this.

Know this part of me.

As a tear tracked down my cheek, I said, "I hurt you, and I'm sorry. I know I ruined our chance of friendship, our chance of something more then. I know I used you." He made to speak, but I shook my head, ignoring the lone tear that had escaped. "PTSD doesn't look a certain way. I don't worry about getting in a car. Shit, I was rear-ended a while back and was fine, but I have bouts where I can become… possessive, unreasonable.

And it's not healthy. But I'm managing it. I'm talking about it, and I'm refusing to let it rule my life anymore."

My therapy sessions were no longer regularly scheduled. My doc had been happy for me to get a new appointment when I felt the need to do so. After I'd screwed Lawrence over, I'd had three months of intense and eye-opening sessions. I believed I was better for it.

At least I hoped I was.

In the next moment, Lawrence scooted over into my space and held my hand, squeezing gently. "I forgive you." He then took me by surprise and stood, tugging me up with him.

Instead of releasing my hand, he used it to pull me toward him. With an inhale, I leaned against him and circled his waist with my arms. His head pressed lightly against mine, his arms wrapping around my back. A loud exhale tore out of me at the comfort from Lawrence's reassuring touch.

I couldn't even remember the last hug I'd received. I'd given them to Georgia and the boys. But this one right here was just for me.

"Thank you," I whispered.

His lips pressed down on my head, soothing me. I closed my eyes at the gesture. "Anytime." A gentle hand caressed my back, the firmness of his casted arm making me smile. This could have been the moment to pull away, but damn, the man knew how to hug. Shamelessly, I snuggled deeper against Lawrence, taking everything I could.

"I think you should finish off that water and head to bed."

I nodded against him, sure he was right, but not quite ready to relinquish the hold we had on each other. Lawrence seemed to know this, as he tightened his grip a fraction. Maybe he needed this as much as I did. One day, I was certain he'd share more with me about his past, just like I had with him. I was okay that it wasn't now.

There was only so much sharing a guy could have in a lifetime, let alone a few weeks.

After feeling able to pull away, I did so, feeling better—still ridiculously drunk and not quite sure if I'd be spending the night in the bathroom, but feeling more together than I had in a long time.

"Ready for bed?" Lawrence asked me, just a few inches between us.

It would be easy to lean in, go for a kiss, but I'd been drunk and upset eight months back, and there was no way I'd be duplicating that. Instead, I dragged my gaze away from Lawrence's tempting mouth and nodded.

"Bed sounds good." I realized I was squinting a little to keep him in focus. It was definitely time for me to face-plant on my mattress.

After staggering to my room and bouncing my shoulder on the wall a few times, I stood smiling, drunkenly so, as Lawrence helped strip me to my boxers and get into bed.

"You think you can make it to the bathroom if you need to hurl?"

I nodded, head against the pillow. "Be okay."

He seemed to hesitate as he hovered by the side of the bed. "Okay. I'll leave the door open, though, so it's less work, just in case."

"'Kay," I mumbled.

"Night, Billy." His voice was closer than I expected, and the small touch to my head, perhaps a kiss, explained why.

"Thanks for making today better." My words were mumbled and slurred, but I thought clear enough for him to understand.

Lawrence's "Anytime" as he left my room brought a smile to my lips before sleep pulled me under.

CHAPTER TEN

FRESH AIR AND THE WHISPER OF A BREEZE HAD NEVER felt so good on my bare skin. Twisting my wrist first, then my healed foot, then both together, I grinned. "I can't tell you how good this feels." I glanced at Billy, whose focus remained on me, his own smile wide.

In the past couple of weeks, Billy and I had grown closer, to the point that other than when he worked, we were inseparable. Each meal we shared, time talking, taking slow walks around the park… every single moment, we got to know each other that much better.

While my own past beyond the tidbits about me and my sister and a few stories of school remained largely unspoken, he'd let me know that he'd be ready to listen when I was ready to tell him. It was that moment that I'd decided that when I was cast-free and able to take full advantage of my freedom, I'd stop this dance between us once and for all.

Billy had worked his way into my heart, and all without sharing a kiss I was desperate for, beyond the one just after the New Year.

"The doc said not to overdo it though. You have to build up your strength."

I grinned, even though the truth of his words put a little bit of a damper on my desire to go for a run. "So no parkour? I was going to suggest I take you out to one of my familiar haunts."

The shake of his head didn't hide his humor. "No parkour. Jesus, Lawrence, don't you dare."

"You know, that just sounds like a challenge to me." I bounced my brows up and down.

"How about you head out with me to take Penny for a walk instead?"

Amusement thrummed through me. "You know that's how I ended up incapacitated for six weeks, right? Coming to the rescue of Penny?"

He rolled his eyes and reached out and took my hand in his, a gesture I loved and that continued to take me by surprise. Billy had been holding my hand at every opportunity possible over the past two weeks. The simple action had my heart racing every time...

and still without the second attempt at a first kiss I eagerly awaited.

"You didn't have me with you last time."

I nudged against him. "I'm not sure I need a protector, but it's kinda hot."

"Perfect. Any chance of making you think I'm irresistible, I'm down for."

I risked a glance at him, heart catching in my throat when his gaze connected with mine. He pulled me up short, gaze heated, lips right there so close to mine.

The world continued around us as we stood in the outpatient parking lot, almost a haze, a blur as I zeroed in on his mouth.

It was time to seize the moment.

"I'm going to kiss you now." Loud and clear, my words rang out, not quite a challenge but a clear assertion of my need to have his mouth on mine.

A smirk I hadn't seen before graced his mouth—a combination of cocky and sweet and absolutely welcoming. And when I stepped closer to him, his gaze didn't falter.

Warm, fresh breath brushed against me. Goose bumps sprung over my skin, extra sensitive on my newly exposed arm. And then his mouth crashed down onto mine.

So much for me kissing him.

The errant thought escaped, disappearing a mere second after his demanding mouth pressed against my own. The brush of his tongue, the feel of his hand touching my back, it drove me to part my mouth and welcome him in. I drew him closer.

Billy taking control was hot, but I needed my fill too. I'd waited seemingly forever for this.

An impatient moan escaped me when he eased away, and somehow, I managed not to hold on, remembering our surroundings. It was quiet, but the two of us kissing under the small canopy of trees beside Billy's car wasn't the best place for this. Especially as the desire to tug him close and kiss a trail over the barely there scruff of his chin rode me hard.

"You about ready for that walk?"

Saying no wasn't really an option, not when a dog needing a walk was on the cards, but the temptation to shake my head and recommend us heading back to his place for more kissing was on the tip of my tongue. And from the heat in Billy's eyes, I expected he'd be up for option B too. But I was certain there'd be time for more.

"Let's go get Penny." The wanting more kisses afterward was added with a silent plea and a small peck to Billy's lips, letting him know this was far from the last we'd share today.

The bob of his head followed as he unlocked the car and we got in.

We drove in silence, my hand in his, my thoughts drifting between the kiss, what came next, and also my relief at having my casts off and being able to head back to work tomorrow, all limbs intact.

Once we'd collected Penny, we headed to the dog park and strolled around, throwing her a tennis ball and talking about building the strength back in my arm and foot. It had been years since my last break, so I understood the importance of slow and steady, but it didn't deter my excitement for being active again.

"And your leg injury, it means no running or jumping out of planes, right?"

"I can run, or jog maybe. A plane jump, not so much. I've made peace with it, I suppose," Billy said. "It's my eye I have to have regular checks for."

I nodded. When Billy had been injured in the collision that had taken Clark's life, he'd nearly lost his sight. His retina had detached, and nerve damage had impacted his vision. After multiple surgeries, his eyes had been saved, but the sight in his right eye was less than 50 percent. The injury had taken me by surprise, as I'd never suspected he had an issue.

"I need to head for another appointment soon, as my left eye isn't quite as strong as it used to be." His nose scrunched up.

"You don't like glasses?"

He sighed as we continued walking around the park. "I'm sure you'd look sexy as hell if you wore glasses," he said, side-eyeing me. "For me, it's just another sign of my body telling me it's in charge."

While there was a lightness in his voice, I recognized the serious undertone.

"I have no doubt you'll pull off glasses and can handle the whole studious look. It's hot." I rubbed against his shoulder. "I just think we keep doing what we can to make sure we're in the best shape possible. If that means our body needs help every now and then, so be it."

"So says the ridiculously fit twenty-seven-year-old."

I laughed. "Yeah, broken bones and all. I know my parkour days are coming to an end," I said wistfully. "I'm not looking forward to the day, but it is what it is. I'll still run until that slows to a jog."

"You're right, and perhaps before you're at full strength, you can do some of those jogs with me before you out-lap me."

I liked the sound of that. Spending time with Billy

doing something I loved sounded like my idea of awesome.

We finished up Penny's walk and dropped her back at Austin's before making our way back home. As we pulled up into the drive, my gaze landed on a black SUV in the driveaway. "Who's that?" I asked, not recognizing the car.

"No idea." Billy pulled up in front of the garage door and stepped out of the car. I followed suit, eyes on the SUV.

The door opened, and my world tilted.

Mario.

"What's wrong?"

Billy's question dragged my gaze to him, and I realized I'd either made a sound or had perhaps been struck wide-eyed and mute.

My mouth opened, and I struggled with how to proceed.

"You know him?"

I nodded, then glanced over at Mario. Now out of the vehicle, he'd walked toward the front and waited, his dark brown eyes fixed on me. Uncertainty filled their depths, something I would have liked to grasp onto, but shaken, I could barely think straight, let alone feel a quiet victory that Mario didn't know what to expect from me.

Billy was the first to speak. "What can I help you with?" Controlled and even, Billy's voice took on that cop tone I'd never heard before. It was enough to break me from my shock. Taking action, I moved to his side, deliberately pressing my shoulder against his, drawing strength from the contact.

Mario had watched my progress, gaze flicking over me, darting between Billy and me. His focus finally landed on Billy, and he offered a polite smile. Ten years ago, even the smallest of smiles from Mario had been enough to make my head spin.

Today, not so much.

"I'm here to see Lawrence." Mario's eyes darted to mine. "Can we talk in private?"

I held his eyes before turning to look at Billy. "Give me five. I won't be long."

Gratitude swept through me when Billy nodded without question, and when he followed with a brief kiss, I wondered how he'd known his reaction was exactly what I needed.

"Call me if you need me."

"Will do, but I'm good. Five minutes. I won't be long." Determination was a heady thing. Mario had left me to the wolves ten years ago. There were no take-backs in life, especially on things that changed the course of my life forever.

Billy left us to it with a hard stare at Mario. I smirked inwardly at his reaction, liking how he balanced his need to protect with my wishes for space. Once he was inside, the door remaining open, I turned my full attention to Mario.

"You look really good, Laurie."

The childhood nickname had me straightening my spine. "Why are you here?" There wasn't a chance I'd put up with small talk.

Mario's shoulders sagged a fraction, but he had no right to any other reaction from me. "I was ordered to hand-deliver this to you." He reached into the car, removing an envelope. I didn't take a step.

"What is it?"

"A wedding invitation."

Surprise rippled through me. Not at all what I was expecting. While I was more than aware of the upcoming wedding, that I was invited didn't make a lick of sense.

"Your mother insisted I get this in your hands and told me to remind you of the implications should you refuse to attend."

A snort tore out of me. Now that was an order I expected. Dangling my sister over my head was one said implication. The other, no doubt, was finding a way for me to be run out of town, all in the aim of nobody knowing my association with the woman who'd birthed me. "Why's she want me there?"

Mario winced before saying, "Your sister mentioned you in an interview. The press caught on to an offhand comment. I think your mom tried hard to suppress it," he answered, and I didn't doubt he spoke the truth.

"I imagine she tried her hardest to erase me completely." My tone was matter-of-fact. Long ago I'd laid to rest any resentment or hurt. Melissa Crawford didn't deserve any emotion from me beyond indifference.

Mario's silence was enough of an answer to let me know that I was right.

"Wouldn't it be easier to make up an excuse?" I didn't wait for his response before asking, curious, "Is that a plus-one invitation?" The reality was I had a choice here, regardless of her threats. The chance to see my sister in the flesh was too much of a temptation to ignore.

A short nod was my answer, and I smiled. "She knows I'll be bringing a guy for a date, right?"

"I expect so."

"Fine. RSVP plus one." I stepped toward him and took the outstretched envelope. Bravado rode me hard with every step and every moment Mario was close by.

"Wait, Lawrence." His grip was firm on my forearm.

My step faltered. "Get your hand off me."

He released me as though he'd been burned and hung his head. "I'm sorry. You know I had no other choice. She—"

"There's always another choice," I said, my voice low, steady. "I was seventeen fucking years old."

Mario edged away from me, his brown skin a deep shade of red.

The years hadn't been kind to Mario. Wrinkles around his eyes were pronounced despite him being only thirty-one. Etched in his eyes was a hollowness I imagined was there from forced proximity to the poison of my mother.

This was the man who'd professed to adore me. This was the man who'd made promises he'd later set in flames. This was the man who'd outed me in a round-about way to my mother, sealing my future and putting me in a car to the airport, exiled from my family.

He was a fucking coward.

Putting one foot in front of the other, I focused on the front door, knowing inside was safety and a man who asked nothing from me. Instead, he gave me everything I needed. Smiles and support and a connection that made my heart pound double time.

While I didn't know what my mother's intention was, what political game she was playing, I'd do what I could to see my sister safe and ensure she was protected as much as I could. But that was me making a choice, and with my sister wanting me by her side, it was not my mother pulling the strings.

Not this time.

By the time I closed the door behind me and heard the engine start, then the SUV drive away, exhaustion beat against me, blurring my vision as a killer headache formed.

"Painkillers?"

I glanced up at Billy. He stood in the hallway a few feet before me. My smile was tight when I nodded. "Yeah, that'd be great, thanks."

For a few beats, his gaze roamed over me, but no questions were fired my way, no demand for answers. Instead, he bobbed his head, instructed me to take a shower, and told me he'd leave the headache tablets in my room with some water.

Gone was the ease of this morning, the simple pleasure of celebrating my freedom from my casts. But despite that, my tight smile loosened, became genuine as I watched him turn back to the kitchen where he kept the first aid kit.

A hot shower helped loosen my tense muscles and push away the darkness impinging my vision. What it didn't stop was the memory of the day my one miserable life was exchanged for another. This one bittersweet in many ways.

From fifteen years old, I'd been convinced Mario was my one and only—hindsight taught me otherwise. Sheltered and all but under house arrest due to Mother's political ambitions and her determination to not allow me to embarrass her, the only respite I had was at school, hiding out in our large gardens, and zipping around the tennis court on my skateboard.

Our gardener, Luis, was a good man and used to let me hide away and hang out with him, much to the disgruntlement of his son, Mario.

And that was how it had started.

Me crushing on him, following him around like a lost puppy.

Me idolizing the guy, even when he was a prick.

Me losing my virginity to Mario in the tool shed in the darkness of night while an icy blast traveled from the north.

And me experiencing betrayal that led to me being sent away to boarding school for the final year of my education, with explicit instructions to never set foot in Wisconsin again.

I stepped out of the shower and toweled off. It was far from late, but my bed beckoned. I slipped under the sheets clean, with still-damp hair, and headache tablets in my system.

The sound of Billy moving through the house was soothing, helping to calm my nerves and irritation.

Seeing my mother again was the last thing I wanted to do. But my sister? That I had the opportunity to see her, especially on her wedding day, was a diversion I could get on board with.

"Hey." Billy's deep voice was hushed. My gaze found his where he stood in the doorway, leaning against the frame. "Feeling any better?"

I managed a smile. "Yeah, thanks."

"Good." He pushed away from the frame, making to leave.

"You want to lie with me for a while?" I asked, maybe too eagerly, but with my emotions causing havoc, my obvious need to be close to him was the least of my worries.

A head bob followed his moving feet as Billy stepped fully into the room, making his way around to the other side of the bed.

When he cast his gaze down at me, drinking me in,

the suggestion easily slipped past my lips. "I'm just in my boxers." The statement pretty easy to read.

Without a word, he stripped, exposing smooth skin on his stomach and a splattering of hairs on his chest. Billy was gorgeous. Plain and simple. And I was lucky as hell to have not only found him but to have built this friendship with him too. It was strange how some things worked out—my accident being one of them. A wayward thought made me think of Ted talking about me and karma. A lightness eased into me at the idea.

And as he pulled back the sheets and slid onto the mattress next to me, my belief was plain as day. The six weeks of broken bones had been an absolute blessing, bringing me to this moment.

There was nothing tentative about Billy's movement when he turned on his side to face me and reached out.

With the palm of his hand pressed against my cheek, he lazily stroked his thumb across my skin. My breath caught at the tenderness of the touch. The gentle affection wasn't what I'd prepared for, but I welcomed the connection. I wanted this to happen too much. Wanted him. Billy. An honest-to-God sigh escaped me as his caress stole my ability to think or do anything but be in this moment.

Concern captured in his gaze when he asked, "Are

you really okay?" I nodded in response as he continued, "You don't have to pretend with me, or hold back."

I smiled, the intensity of his words warming me from inside out. I focused on how his lips tugged upward, reacting to me. "I really am. Sometimes the past just creeps on up and likes to jump out at me, you know? And this time was one hell of a wake-up call. I know there's no escaping it, outrunning it, and that's okay." I pulled away from him, away from his gentle touch. These touches we'd been sharing lately were so incredibly good and becoming the best part of my day. Connection was one thing, but it was specifically Billy I craved being close to.

Awareness shot through me when he trailed his rough fingers down my cheek, over my itchy beard I really should shave, and my neck. My heartbeat increased, my breathing following the same pattern.

"Do you need me to do something for you?"

Dragging my bottom lip into my mouth, I couldn't help but think of the many ways Billy could help me. Practically every scenario involved his mouth crushed to mine, his lips on my skin. The temptation was there, but was it wise with my emotions scattered like autumn leaves in the breeze? I had no clue at this point.

"Can you just lie with me for a while?" There was no hiding the need in my voice, but over the past few weeks, we'd come so far that revealing myself to him no longer worried me. I mulled over the words bouncing around in my head. My heart had implanted them there, but to speak them would change everything.

But then there was the kiss earlier in the parking lot.

I huffed out a breath before going for it. "All I need is you." I didn't elaborate, didn't bumble through with an explanation. What was the point?

After all that had happened, it was finally time to trust in myself and what I was feeling.

My gaze locked with his. His startling eyes were intense, filled with so many emotions it could take me a lifetime to unravel them all. When he leaned forward, his mouth close to mine, I angled slightly in clear invitation. "Kiss me." My words were barely out before his mouth slanted over mine.

On contact, my eyelids fluttered closed, and I brushed my tongue against his lips. Caution was far in the rearview mirror. Uncertainty took a back seat as I gave him everything. Billy's hold on me was firm, possessive as our mouths connected—all heat and fire. He swept his tongue against mine as our lips parted against one another's. Wings took flight in my chest, making it hard to breathe, to think, but there was no way I was ready to come up for air. Sweet heat came alive, setting fire to those wings and lighting me up when his boxer-clad groin rubbed against me. I groaned into the kiss, the touch, the feel of his body, luxuriating in the rightness of the moment.

The kiss was familiar.

Hot.

Effortless.

Everything about the connection was flawless, natural.

I drew in a shaky breath and pulled away, a smile lifting my lips. "This okay?"

Billy's laugh was deep, startling, and brightened his eyes, making it even harder to pull away from how they ensnared me. "More than. The best," he said. The words were punctuated by a gentle kiss. "You happy for some more?"

"Hell yes."

The smile playing on his lips remained but a beat before his mouth reconnected. Doing what felt right and good, I lifted my left leg and wrapped it around his hip. Billy's moan of appreciation set off a new spark of need, and I angled my hips, seeking out friction.

Needing his skin against mine, eager for his weight, I tugged and urged him on top of me, my thighs parting before I held on tightly with them. This… *this* was fucking perfect. His solid weight felt right, his kisses deep and grounding, and when he groaned once again, I promised myself right then I'd work my ass off to make this work out between us.

With my palms on his ass, I pulled him toward me, grinding, rutting, absorbing each movement, sensation traveling from my dick to every nerve in my body. Every emotion I had for Billy I poured into our kiss. For the past year, we could have had this.

But I refused to live with what-ifs.

I wasn't a man who believed in fate or destiny—even though karma was my new best friend. But I recognized some things happened for a reason, and I had to believe that the moment was right this time around. Close to unraveling, I held tight, enjoying his need, hard and hot against my groin.

Wanting more, needing my boxers off, I made to pull away. I needed to tell him we had to be naked right now, let him know I'd added condoms and lube to the bedside drawer, hoping like hell we'd get to this point one day. As if sensing I planned to pull away, he deepened the kiss, apparently not liking that at all. His grip tightened, hands moving to my hips, fingers dipping under the waistband of the material between us.

I *needed* action. Needed it all.

And holy shit, I was desperate but didn't give a damn at this point. Not so close to getting my fill.

Disconnecting, our eyes met. "Condoms and lube." I reached out to the table, gaze still connected with his. I fumbled, struggled to find purchase with the handle.

"Let me."

I nodded emphatically, happy for him to take over. As he reached for the handle, I lifted my head, lips brushing against his neck. I licked, nibbled, inhaled the scent that was uniquely his.

"Got it. You want to put this on, or shall I?"

That he didn't assume, didn't simply take the lead had a new wave of desire spiraling through me. "I'm good for you to top, but the thought of you riding me…." I trailed off, shivering as that same desire hit hard, making me throb and my asshole twitch. "Get inside me."

"I can do that." Lifting his body away, he circled a rough finger over one of my nipples. "You want my mouth on you first?"

"After," I answered breathily, hardly recognizing my own voice.

"Even if you come with me buried inside you?"

A fresh shudder of desire had my groan escaping. "Never come like that before."

He raised his brow, and I was sure he was thinking about when we'd been together all of those months ago. That time I'd come with his mouth on me too. Intensity flashed through his eyes, and I grinned. "You seeing that as a challenge now, huh?"

He laughed lightly. "Just maybe."

"Good." I wanted this to matter, wanted him to see me shatter, and I would love to do that while he hit hard against my prostate.

A crackle of energy pulsed between us as he opened the lube, preparing himself before opening me up. My gasping breaths, his words of encouragement, and the sound of wet fingers working against my hot, tight skin filled the room. The combination was the sexiest sound I'd ever heard.

Billy's mouth returned to mine as his fingers worked me over, his other hand stroking across my waist. Once he pulled away, his gaze seared mine. I couldn't concentrate, couldn't focus. Between the bite of pain, the rush of pleasure as he stroked inside me, and the desire in his eyes, I latched on to the only thing I could.

Literally.

His cock.

Wide-eyed, Billy caught his breath, his eyes blazing. Clinging to his reaction, luxuriating in my hold on him, I pulled myself together enough to grin, low laughter rumbling out of me. "I need this now."

His fingers delved deeper, causing me to bite down on my bottom lip before he removed them completely. "You want this?"

I wanted it all.

His lips, his tongue, his fingers, him. Truly everything. Coherent thoughts fled as he brushed against me, wrapped his hand around mine, and pushed against my opening. Gripping my hand, he removed it from his covered cock and placed it on his waist, while his traveled to the outside of my thigh. "Just you. I want you. Want it all."

Billy's soft smile captured my attention. He then nodded, repositioned himself, and slowly entered.

Filled up and gasping, I slammed my eyelids closed. It had been a while. "Fuck!" I cried, the word garbled as I gripped my legs around his waist tighter.

"You good?" His gentle words lit with concern had me opening my eyes.

"Yeah," I said. "Just been a while."

"You want me to st—"

"Don't even think of finishing that sentence." His

dick twitched at that, making me groan. "I need you to move."

He bobbed his head, his gaze never drifting from mine.

The last time we'd been together had been incredible, even with the sloppiness of drunkenness, but this, with the intensity in his eyes, my affection for Billy riding me hard, was so much more.

He moved, building speed, changing the discomfort to a hit of pleasure. We worked together, rocking back and forth. Me pushing against him, chasing the connection and wanting him as deep as possible.

"That's it," he all but growled as he changed the angle and rocked into me harder. "Fuck, so good." I couldn't even nod in agreement. Every movement offered the promise of sweet release. I was lost, adrift, and not quite sure I would survive the force of the pleasure building every time he touched that place inside me that sent stars into my vision.

I gasped when his hand made contact with my cock. With my eyes wide open, a tremble ripped through me. A shot of pleasure hit my balls, my gut, my brain, sending my nerves into overdrive. My release had me tensing, calling out, my goddamn toes curling. As the sensation rushed through my body, pleasure rolled through me as I spilled onto his hand and my stomach.

Billy's garbled cry followed when I contracted around him in a vise grip. He shuddered and cried out in release; my eyes opened just enough to witness the bliss on his face. The hold he had on me didn't loosen, didn't falter for a beat as he recaptured his breath, his eyes finally opening, gaze finding mine.

He released his firm grip and leaned down, capturing my mouth. Not an inch of space between us remained as his tongue parted my lips and invaded. I welcomed the intrusion, holding Billy close.

Both breathless, we eased out of the kiss, smiling.

"I've never been happier to be proven wrong," I said, high from the rush of coming with him inside me.

He laughed. "I like a good challenge. Keep them coming." He followed with a small kiss, seeming reluctant when he pulled away, saying, "I suppose we should clean up."

"Another shower, this one with you, sounds good."

Brightening at my words, he smiled. "I'm more than happy with that plan."

Billy eased out of me. As he held the full condom in place, he watched me intently. I wondered how quickly it would take for him to get hard again. I'd still yet to taste him. The thought made me smile, and Billy's eyebrow quirked high at my reaction.

"What's that smile for?"

I shrugged. "Just thinking I could help you clean up."

"Is that right?"

"Yeah, with my tongue."

The darkening of eyes was heady and had me scrambling. "I'll meet you in your shower," I said, already at the doorway, snickering when I heard Billy fumbling behind me in his haste.

CHAPTER ELEVEN

BILLY

IT WAS THE FOLLOWING DAY THAT LAWRENCE HANDED me an opened envelope. I smiled, taking it off him despite his more somber expression. I was still in a euphoric haze of post-orgasmic bliss, my fourth in twenty-four hours, my happy glow surrounding me. But I knew what he was handing me was to do with that guy Mario who'd been here yesterday. So it was necessary to pull my head away from the thoughts of my mouth on Lawrence's skin and give him the attention he deserved.

"This what he gave you yesterday?" I asked, wanting confirmation.

"Yeah. Ordered to hand-deliver it."

My brows dipped low, his choice of words piquing

my interest and sending a shot of uncertainty to my nerve endings.

Fragments of his past were all Lawrence had shared so far, and I was okay with that, certain he'd tell me what I needed to know or what he wanted me to. I assumed from the calligraphy script of his name on the front of the pristine white envelope, the doors were being thrown wide open.

A wedding invitation sat in my hands. It was fancy, the paper expensive. I recognized his sister's name and saw she was marrying a guy called Harry Ludlow. The place for the parents' names had just one—Melissa Crawford. The name didn't mean anything to me beyond the shared last name with Lawrence.

"You knew your sister was getting married, right?" I asked, trying to recall one of our conversations about her over the past few weeks. "Didn't you say she was young, twenty-one?" It seemed too young, but what did I know?

"Yeah," he answered with a nod. "We don't chat much, but regularly enough for me to know she was engaged. Harry seems nice, and she thankfully seems in love and happy." A casual shrug followed.

"And that's a surprise? Isn't that usually the reason why people get married?"

The humorless laugh sounded hollow coming from

Lawrence. He sat next to me with a heavy sigh, angling on the couch, his knee brushing my thigh. "I suppose I need to explain who my mom is."

I bobbed my head and mirrored his position, facing him properly.

"Melissa Crawford, my mom, is the governor of Wisconsin."

I appreciated his pause, needing the moment for his words to sink in. And while they did, nothing I knew made sense. Lawrence was the son of a governor, scraping by on a bartender's wages, relying on tips, and enjoyed fucking parkour in his spare time.

With no idea how to respond or which of the many questions to ask first, I started with the simple direction, "Explain."

"The condensed version okay? Not sure I have it in me to hash everything out right now."

"Of course."

"When I was seventeen, I was caught with Mario…." His nose crinkled, heat suffusing his cheeks before he clarified, "I was sucking him off."

Already I had a fair idea that I wasn't going to like this story, and with that information, I expected I'd be looking for a chance to punch Mario. I kept silent, focused and listening, giving Lawrence the room to speak without interruption.

"Long story short, Mario said I seduced him, called me a 'fag.'" Lawrence air quoted, and I sneered at the word but still held back from speaking. "Mom sent me to a boarding school for the last year of high school a few states away, refused to let me come home, and cut off communication from my sister. Her focus was keeping her good name and apparently protecting my sister too. Said she'd have Mario arrested for statutory rape since I was underage, get his dad deported back to Mexico, despite him being completely legal." He shook his head. "In hindsight, the latter was probably bullshit, but I was seventeen and terrified.

"She wasn't governor then, gay marriage certainly wasn't legal, and my mom had no room for a gay son who apparently couldn't keep his mouth to himself. Said that if I came back, caused a stir, grabbed any single bit of attention, it would impact my sister the most. Threatened her inheritance, her social standing." He shook his head, distaste clear as day on his features. "My sister wouldn't be able to cope in the real world. She's not academic, not street smart, but she's sweet and lovely." Lawrence's voice softened when he spoke of his sister, his love for her clear.

He continued, saying, "As soon as I found out about Mary's wedding, I searched for any information on the guy she's getting married to, and he seems legit. Don't get me wrong, Mom wouldn't approve if his family weren't at least financially well off, and even better if they were politically influential, but from what I can tell, Harry works hard and loves my sister."

He huffed out a breath, and I wasn't sure if he was finished or not. His gaze was intent when he said, "I've never been able to settle anywhere for long. I know Mom runs checks on me every few months or so, perhaps has alerts or some shit so she can squash anything that may threaten public opinion."

Understanding registered, and I said, "That's why you didn't want to file a police report."

"Yeah. Even though I wasn't at fault, if the story hit the press, my name would be on the internet in an article somewhere."

I shook my head, trying to comprehend his story. "But what has she been telling everyone all this time, the past ten years?"

Bitterness crossed his features. The sight hurt my heart, and the seed of anger planted in my gut as soon as his story started sprouted roots and started to grow something fierce.

"My sister, and I suppose everyone else, believes I went to Canada for college and stayed there after graduating."

"And you kept up with the pretense all this time… and have been alone?"

He bobbed his head, jaw tight as he did so. "It is what it is. I communicate with my sister—pretty sure my mom intercepts my birthday cards to Mary and probably throws on a fucking Canadian stamp," he said with a snort, "and go about living my life the best way I can."

"And you not settling?" Beyond everything, my selfish interests sparked to life. I didn't want Lawrence to move on. We had something amazing going, and I didn't want to lose that.

"The last place I lived was for about six months. That was before I was rear-ended by a car. It was outside a police station, unbelievably. I managed to deal with the collision without claiming on insurance, but two weeks later, I was fired from my job. Apparently, I'd been getting complaints, which is total bullshit."

I shook my head in disbelief as he continued. He told me about incidents where he was threatened, or lost his rental, lost his job, forcing him to move on and leave town.

"And you think your mom is responsible for this, the governor of Wisconsin?" I clarified. Disbelief rippled through me, right alongside my horror. That his mom prevented him from making a home and becoming a local face so she could protect her image was a bastard of a thing. I'd seen corruption when I was a detective, so I believed that all Lawrence's "bad luck" wasn't simply fate but politically motivated. But the lengths she went to made my blood boil.

Selfishness was one thing, but she was fucking cruel.

"You're incredible." The fierceness of my words was undeniable as I reached out and pressed my palm to his bristly cheek.

Wide-eyed and blushing, Lawrence smiled. "You think?" Confusion lifted his words into a clear question.

"I know," I clarified. "That you've stayed sane, and honest, and so…" I grasped for the words, struggling to voice just how remarkable I thought Lawrence was before landing on, "… you." The "you" had him laughing. "You really are an amazing man." I sealed my words with a kiss, needing the connection, desperate to show him what a wonder he was, words not doing justice.

The kiss was met with passion and heat. Fire licked through me when his tongue touched mine. I pushed him back, making quick work of straddling him. I didn't stop, my kisses relentless, breathing choppy. I eased back when my lungs strained for fresh breath.

"I think you're incredible too," Lawrence said, the words passing his kiss-swollen lips and making me smile. He studied me intently for a few beats, our breathing the only sound before he tentatively asked, "Will you come with me to the wedding?"

As he'd opened up to me about his past, I'd assumed, *hoped* that would be the case. "Yes." My answer was immediate, but I parted my lips, showing my hesitation.

"Are you following up with a *but*?"

I remained on his lap as I spoke, not willing to sever this moment. "Yeah, there's a but." Lawrence deflated before my eyes, so I quickly added, "I'll go with you, absolutely. I want to go with you, support you, be your plus one." I smiled at that, genuinely thrilled he was thinking about the future, anticipating that in three weeks' time, there was no uncertainty we'd be together. "The *but* is really a warning," I admitted, figuring it was easier to simply share my concerns. "I don't know if I'll be able to keep my mouth shut."

Understanding registered in his eyes. "Mario."

I nodded, saying, "And your mom. If she even goes so far as to look at you the wrong way—"

Lawrence's pointer finger against my lips cut me off. My brows lifted in surprise, my smile quickly mimicking his when it was clear he wasn't pissed at me.

"Is this the protective side you were talking about?"

I shrugged. "Yeah, but it's also me as a gay man who doesn't suffer bigoted assholes easily, or deceitful bastards for that matter either."

He lost his smile, and I immediately wanted it back. He went on to say, "Thank you for saying you'll come. It means a lot. I don't want my sister's big day ruined though."

"I get it. I do, and I promise I won't do that to her or to you. But if something happens, I don't think I'll be able to let it slide. But I promise it won't be in front of your sister. I'll bite my tongue if she's around."

"And then lay into whatever asshat's pissed you off later?"

"Exactly." My tone lightened as I pushed humor into my response. "You see, you didn't even know me when I had a badge, but you understand how I work."

The laughter that followed eased my shoulders. I seriously wouldn't tire of hearing Lawrence's deep chortle. "I bet you were hot when in uniform," he said, peering up at me, his hands squeezing my backside.

Pleased we'd moved on from the more serious

topic, a smile stretched my mouth wide. It didn't mean we wouldn't be revisiting it, but for now, this was what Lawrence needed. I was good with that.

"Mr. January in the charity calendar five years in a row." I bounced my eyebrows up and down for effect, pulling another laugh from him.

"I bet you were. Is the uniform something you had to give back, or if I rummage around, is it something I'll find covered in dust bunnies?"

"I may have a uniform lying around."

His eyes lit up, interest evident. "One day, that's something I would love."

My smile was soft. It had been years since I'd donned a uniform, especially since I'd been in plain clothes for three years before my busted leg and damaged eye. "One day we can definitely arrange that."

***

The more I researched Melissa Crawford, the more I loathed her. But in doing so, I thought I'd figured out the main reason she was agreeing to accommodate her daughter by bringing Lawrence into the fold.

It was close to election time, and likely the last chance to pull Lawrence out of hiding before anyone else did. I imagined ensuring his outing happened on her terms was the main mission. No doubt there were also other political reasons too.

Lawrence's arms wrapping around my shoulders startled me, causing him to laugh. He kissed my cheek before saying, "Thanks for letting me borrow your car."

I tilted my head back, smiled, and hoped he'd take the hint. A moment later, his lips connected with mine. "No worries," I said when he pulled away. "Your shift go okay?"

He bobbed his head and walked around the sofa to sit by my side, his thigh touching mine. I picked up the remote and turned the TV off. Not that I'd been really watching the show. My head was full of the wedding taking place this weekend and our journey tomorrow.

"It was fine. Surprisingly busy for a Wednesday. Biscuit helped me out. Got me a load of tips too."

I grinned at the mention of Ted and Jason's cute puppy. "I bet. He's pretty adorable. Not sure I fancy myself as a Lab man though."

"Hell no," Lawrence said, his eyes narrowing. "There's no such thing as *not* a Lab man. Everyone likes Labradors. They're too cute not to." He followed up by flexing his fingers in my side.

My snort was abrupt as I grabbed onto his

offending fingers that had done too good a job of finding their mark in my ticklish spot. "Hey, I didn't say he wasn't a good-looking dog, but I just never imagined owning one."

With his eyes still narrowed and hand still in mine, he asked, "So what sort of dog would you like?"

I shrugged. "Maybe a Chinook or a German shepherd."

Lawrence's mock frown finally disappeared, and he smiled. "Both nice dogs. You want a dog then?"

"A couple for sure. The yard's big. It's not like we're not active and wouldn't be happy to head out for walks whenever possible."

Stiff-limbed, Lawrence seemed to stop breathing. And I knew exactly why. There was nothing accidental about my word choice. The length of time the two of us had known each other, regardless of us becoming an official couple, was neither here nor there as far as I was concerned.

Truth be told, since almost three weeks ago, he'd slept in my bed every night, despite the decorating now complete in the apartment and the furniture moved back. Most of his clothes had been in the spare room, where they still remained. While I hadn't officially opened up my own closet for him yet, it was just a step away.

"Is that something you want, for us?" he asked.

My gaze searched his, trying to get a read on his reaction. While he didn't look horror-stricken, he wasn't bouncing up and down with the possibility either. I selected my words carefully. "One day for sure. When I moved and bought this place, my focus was on quiet and escape rather than anything more. But perhaps planning for the future was nestled somewhere in the back of my mind at the time."

A soft smile appeared on Lawrence's lips. "It's a great house."

"And what about you. Dogs?" I hesitated before adding, "Kids?"

"Dogs for sure, and kids…." A shrug followed. "My childhood was miserable, and yeah, I'm sure as hell I'd do a better job at parenting. I just don't ever see myself as a dad, you know?"

"I do." I could completely relate to the "not being a parent" opinion, but that was nothing to do with my upbringing. I'd been blessed when it came to family.

"So," he said, his tone changing, "you set for tomorrow?"

If he hadn't told me how much he was dreading the visit, despite his eagerness to see Mary, I would have never known. There was no nuance of dread or excitement in his voice. No physical tells either.

"Yeah. I picked up my suit from the dry cleaners, packed up the bag, and put our tickets on my phone app." I stroked my thumb over his hand. "How you doin'? Gonna be okay?"

The tentative nod this time was more telling. "I suppose. I just hope like hell my mom doesn't get into anything with me, and I have no idea the party line she's going for either. I expect I'll find out Friday morning."

While we flew out to Madison tomorrow, we'd reserved a hotel room and had no plans to see anyone. Lawrence wanted to acclimatize, and no doubt get his head prepared for the busy weekend. I noticed nervous energy start to thrum off him again after the brief interlude, like it had done all week. And once we were in his home state, I could only imagine how wired he'd be.

My own goals this weekend were clear. Protect Lawrence and support him as best as I could.

On the plus side, I was an expected guest. There'd been a whole stack of paperwork sent through from the governor's security team to ensure I could attend the wedding. Being a former cop had made that easier, I was sure. My expectations were low, anticipating cutting looks and sharp tongues. I could handle it all, except for the same being thrown at Lawrence and him being hurt in the process.

Over the past couple of weeks, he'd opened up more about the ten years since he was abandoned. A college fund had been in place for him, but he'd discarded all offers of support and links with his mom. And I couldn't blame him.

It had meant he was on his own, working shitty jobs, living in boarding houses and the like, and even spending some weeks roughing it.

I hadn't exaggerated when I'd told him how incredible he was.

And the more I knew him, more I learned, not only about the past but the man he was today, the more I opened my heart to the guy. He already had a piece of it. I suspected it wouldn't take long for him to own it completely.

"I don't mind being evasive and playing the game," Lawrence said, pulling me from my thoughts. I refocused on him, drinking in every word. "I want to simply be there for my sister and then leave. I don't want to be involved in anything my mother may be strategizing."

I nodded, wondering if he'd deduced as much, as it was an absolute possibility.

"But I won't lie. I've no shame in how I've lived the past ten years."

I squeezed his hand. "Nor should you have," I agreed.

Before he could respond, I tugged him close and wrapped him up in my arms. That I could do this, offer comfort and absorb his closeness, was a heady feeling. I promised myself I'd never take it for granted.

It was only the alert of a text message coming through on my phone that had me pulling away.

"Why don't you deal with that while I go and grab a shower? I have the stink of beer on me."

My lips grazed his before he stood. "It's a scent I'm liking more and more." I threw him a cheesy grin. He gifted me an eye roll in response.

"That's gross. Eau de sweat and beer makes me simply question your good taste." He quirked one eyebrow for good measure and darted away before my palm could swat his ass.

"You can run!" I hollered after him while picking up my phone from the table.

Georgia: I'm planning early. Thanksgiving, your place. Time for you to suck it up and meet Russell, and the kids miss you like crazy.

The flip in my gut was hard to ignore, but I had to do

so. I knew Georgia needed this, perhaps more than I did. It was clear she was serious about this Russell guy, or else a Thanksgiving invite wouldn't be happening; plus it had been at least a year that she'd been dating the guy.

I sighed. It didn't mean it would be easy though. But she was right. I had to suck it up. This was about her and the boys.

Me: Fine. I'll clean the shotgun beforehand.

Georgia: You do that and you'll find a shot in your ass.

I laughed, the sound loud in the quiet living room.

Me: What's this guy do again?

Georgia: This "guy" is a professional MMA fighter.

I paused at that, my brows scrunching together.

Me: WTF! You're not serious?!

Me: Screw the shotgun, I'll look for an auto.

Georgia: You're a dick.

Me: But really, MMA?

After a minute, she still hadn't responded. "She can't be serious," I said aloud to the empty room.

Me: Georgia!!!!!

Georgia: Psych! You're too easy, Hilton. Had you shittin' yourself, though, right?

Amused, I shook my head.

Georgia: He's a counselor.

Huh. I wondered if that's how she'd met him.

Georgia: Works with LGBTQ youth.

Fuck. She just had to go and say that. Georgia knew what she was doing, playing her cards so damn perfectly. I sighed, shaking my head and smiling, albeit begrudgingly.

Me: So what you're saying is I can't hate the guy, huh? Not fair, woman.

Georgia: Well, you could, but that would make you an asshole.

I snorted.

Me: Touché, woman, touché. I'll give him the benefit of the doubt.

Me: Reluctantly.

I really was an asshole at times, but I kept myself entertained.

Georgia: You do that. And the apartment will be free for me and Russell by then, right? Loverboy will be moved in, and you can kid sit. Perfect. Sorted. Got to go. Love you. X

I was laughing again when I headed into the bedroom, walking in on Lawrence drying off.

"What're you laughing about?"

"Georgia," I answered, gaze roaming over his chest before dragging down to his stomach and then lower.

"Eyes up here." Humor lit his voice. My gaze lifted

to meet his, the amusement evident there too. "Everything okay?"

I nodded and stepped into his space, removing the towel from his hands and throwing it to the floor. "Yeah," I said, mouth going for his neck. I pressed kisses along his skin and worked to his chest and his nipple, earning me a sweet groan. As I worked lower, he gripped my shoulders.

"Just yeah?" he asked breathily.

I chuckled. "You want me to answer or do you want your cock in my mouth?"

Fierce intensity spilled into his eyes when our gazes connected.

"Mouth every time."

I smirked before saying, "Thought so," a moment before I brought him to his knees and ensured his mind was filled with nothing but my touch and his pleasure.

CHAPTER TWELVE

LAWRENCE

Needing the combination of comfort and wanting to make my intentions clear that I wasn't hiding our relationship, I reached for Billy's hand as we stepped away from the carousel with our bags. He looked at me as I did so and cast me a wink.

"Signs for a cab point us over there," he said after pausing and taking in our surroundings.

I nodded, gaze drifting around the metal and glass construction. People moved around at speed, most seemingly on a mission. Spending most of my days in small towns over the years, I was no longer accustomed to the hustle and bustle of a city or the noises that came with it.

"Is it bad that I'm already counting the hours till we can head home?" I said, leaning into him as I spoke.

"I'm right there with you. It might be nice to get a decent meal tonight though," he said, smiling and starting for the left where the signs directed us.

"That's true." Over the years, money had been tight, but I was nothing if not resourceful. I'd never pushed my budget, had always saved. It had made taking time off from work a little easier, that and how I had no debt. It meant I'd had just enough for this trip at least, especially when Billy had insisted he'd pay for the three nights' accommodation after I paid for the flights. He'd argued about me paying for his ticket, but the power of persuasion was a newfound skill of mine apparently.

"I think this is for us." Billy's voice startled me and had me looking at him and then following his line of sight. A driver stood with my name on an iPad.

"It seems so." Truth was, I'd half expected this, and rather than fight this interference, I went with the flow. I knew when to fight my battles, and this wasn't one of them.

"Saves us fighting for a cab, right?"

I smiled at Billy's sweetness, his attempt to ease the tension cording my neck. "Right."

As we head for the car, I gave myself a moment to embrace the relief that at least Mario hadn't been sent to collect us. I didn't think Billy would have been quite as accommodating if that had been the case.

"What are you smirking at?" he asked once we were buckled in the back seat of the sleek car.

Not wanting to mention Mario's name and bring unnecessary tension to the conversation, I gave a light shrug, going with "I'm kinda looking forward to exploring the city."

He nodded and reached for my hand, clasping it. "Yeah, me too. Seems crazy that I've never been here before, considering how close I used to live, really."

It was true. Billy had been born and raised in Chicago, just one state over. And funnily, I'd never been to Illinois either. Growing up, I'd led a sheltered existence, and once I'd been out on my own, I didn't want to be so close to my home state.

"Well, we should definitely make the most of it. Try to forget the real shitshow of this weekend." Anxiety gnawed in my chest, pissing me off. I felt out of sorts and completely on edge.

"It'll all work out," Billy said, leaning into me, offering me support. "Remember, I've got your back. You need a getaway car, I'm your man, right?"

I snorted at his sweetness. "You know, at one point I struggled to believe you were a cop," I admitted.

"You did?" Curiosity wrinkled his brows.

"Yeah. I don't know what exactly made it hard, but since getting to know you better, it's easier to imagine."

Billy grinned. "Is this you wanting to blow me when I'm in my uniform? 'Cause you know, I'm warming up to that idea."

I snorted, not quite caring if our words carried despite our quiet voices. "I did not offer to blow you while you were in your blues." Before Billy had time to respond, I leaned in closer, whispering, "But I didn't say I wouldn't."

We continued to talk and look out at the surroundings and the steady traffic as we entered the city. And despite the concern sitting heavily in the pit of my stomach, holding Billy's hand in mine made everything seem a little more bearable. I certainly was able to breathe a little easier too.

Within thirty minutes, we were checking into the hotel. Our room had apparently been upgraded, and the bill taken care of. I didn't even question how she knew where we'd booked a room. This was my mom. Jaw tight, I'd bobbed my head, said my thanks to the guy on reception, and followed the bellman to the elevator. The whole time, Billy remained stoically silent, his grip on mine firm. When I looked at him, he grinned, a genuine tilt of his lips that had me raising my brows and my own lips twitching in response. "What?" I asked quietly.

"I figure this suite will have a huge-ass bath and a pretty impressive bar." He wriggled his brows, making me chuckle. The shift in his eyes was immediate, a glimmer of relief there that I'd taken the bait. He cleared his throat, saying loudly, "So this suite, does it have a walk-in shower, maybe with a bench seat?" He directed his question to the bellman, whose smile remained fixed.

Not a blush was to be seen as he answered without faltering, "I believe the Emerald Suite has a double shower and a marble stone bench seat, yes." He dipped his head and looked away, refocusing on the elevator's closed doors.

Damn, the man had some serious skills. I chuckled and made eye contact with Billy. "That make you happy?"

His gaze dipped to my mouth, the tell his lips would find purchase there. He didn't disappoint as he leaned in for a brief kiss. "The aim is to make you happy."

Emotion clogged my words, preventing them from escaping. And while I'd already expected to be completely under his spell, this moment, him doing all he could for me, without a doubt I knew I loved him. It was as simple as that. As easy as that.

The ping of the elevator dragged my eyes away from Billy's. And not a moment too soon. Confessing my love in an elevator, on a visit from hell, and in front of a bellman wasn't my idea of the best of moments.

After being escorted to our suite, which was modern and comfortable and large, Billy and I lost no time in getting to the hot water. We settled into the large jacuzzi tub to quench the desire he'd stirred in me since entering the hotel.

It was what we both needed. And that he left me feeling boneless and exhilarated helped a helluva lot to chill me out.

Soon after—sated and satisfied—we dressed and headed into the city, hand in hand, and explored the sights. It had been such a long time since I'd been in Madison, and since the last time was with the eyes of a seventeen-year-old, I hadn't truly appreciated how beautiful it was. It was vibrant and pretty and perfectly positioned between two breathtaking lakes.

As far as cities went, it was still arguably my favorite, despite the memories here. And as we wandered the streets after eating pub-cooked food on the water's edge, I felt able to breathe for the first time since the flight.

"You've made today great, thank you." I squeezed Billy's palm that remained clasped in mine.

"I'm glad. It's a nice place."

I nodded. "I still can't believe you used to live in Chicago and never visited here."

He laughed. "I know. It's what, just a couple of hours or so away?" He shrugged. "What can I say other than I worked long hours."

"I can't imagine being a police officer, how hard it was, especially in a city." And I was relieved as hell he no longer was.

"It was my job, what I always wanted to do, you know?"

"Do you miss it?" I spotted a bench overlooking the sparkling water and led Billy toward it, where we sat. I turned slightly to watch him as he spoke.

"I miss the camaraderie, a few of the guys. I suppose I miss those moments where I felt I'd done some good and effected change, but everything else that comes with it…." He shook his head, looking out into the distance. "Yeah, the everything else not so much."

I could only imagine. He'd shared with me the details of the accident, told me the horror story. He also shared with me other stories, some amusing, some having me gripping his hand tightly. He'd mentioned a couple of times how incredible he thought I was. But, no, compared to Billy, I was a blip on the scales. He adamantly argued the point though.

Seeming lost in thought, perhaps a memory of days gone by on the force, Billy became quiet. Not sullen so much as taking a moment. I leaned into him in the silence, appreciating the quiet and being with him.

"How about you? Did you, *do you* have a dream? Was there something you always wanted to do?"

I glanced at him, latching on to his gentle gaze. "This was where I'd always envisioned going to college," I admitted, pointing in the distance toward the imposing building of the University of Wisconsin-Madison. "Even if I hadn't been shipped off, it wouldn't have been allowed. My mother was adamant I was to attend Cornell, where she attended."

He remained silent, giving me the room to speak.

"She had grand plans of me being a surgeon, perhaps a lawyer." I shook my head at the thought of both. "Sometimes I think everything worked out the way it was supposed to, you know?"

"What do you mean?"

"If I'd stayed, I have no doubt I would have been pushed into doing as she asked." I laughed with genuine humor. "Can you imagine me as a surgeon or lawyer?"

Billy joined in and chuckled beside me. "You could have made history as the first surgeon or lawyer who kicked ass at parkour or something. I can't see many in either profession jumping off buildings and somersaulting off walls." He leaned in and tugged on my earlobe with his teeth, whispering, "Is it bad that I think it's kinda hot you do that?"

"You want to see me in action, huh?"

"Damn straight." He angled away so he could meet my gaze. "But if you hurt yourself, I'll kick your ass."

"Ha. Duly noted," I said.

"Good, now back to the question. If you'd gone on to college, what would you have studied?"

I thought back and smiled. "Back then I considered social work or chemistry."

Billy looked at me, wide-eyed. "Well, they're worlds apart."

I shrugged, still grinning. "I was eighteen the last time I even considered college, when I was at boarding school. I was a kid with no real clue other than staying as far away from this place as possible." It was a bittersweet feeling, being back. I luxuriated in the knowledge of being here, was excited as hell to be seeing my sister tomorrow. It was everything else associated with this place that was the problem.

"But I'm happy working in the bar, in the kitchen. Like doing some of the cooking too."

Billy brushed an unruly strand of hair out of my face. It was in need of a cut, which I may have deliberately been avoiding to look a little more unkempt for my mom. "I think you're a great cook. You can pour a mean beer too."

"Thanks. I know it's not a profession in the traditional sense, maybe not even my chosen career at this stage, but it's honest work, and I like it."

"Even with Ted driving you to distraction?" Billy asked, amused.

I chuckled. "Especially with Ted driving me to distraction." It was true. I worked with good, honest people, and in doing so was lucky enough to have been embraced by a community. I didn't need much, and every day over the past eighteen months or so, I'd felt lucky to have stumbled on the small town of Kirkby and the bar. It led me to Billy.

And there was no one I'd prefer to have at my side —at my back too.

"You're young, and it's good that you're happy. It's important. And whether you carry on with what you're doing or want something different later on, you can go for it."

My mouth tilted into a small smile. "You going to tell me the world's my oyster?" I sassed.

His snort followed. "Not now I'm not." His laughter settled into a grin. "But the meaning's there all the same."

After taking in the city and checking out the botanical gardens, we spent the evening eating room service in bed. A car was picking us up at ten the next morning to take us to the Madison Concourse Hotel for a pre-wedding brunch. We'd been encouraged to stay there, too, but I needed a place to escape to should I need it.

The wedding wasn't taking place Saturday afternoon, but since this was no doubt the wedding of the year, considering the governor's daughter was getting married, a whole weekend affair was planned.

I'd considered seeing my sister before tomorrow, but when I'd been able to make contact with her, between her tears of happiness that I'd be attending, she'd talked me through a ludicrous schedule that apparently had to run like clockwork, by order of our mother.

Surprisingly I managed a decent night's sleep. I gave Billy 100 percent credit for settling my nerves by making me scream in pleasure to the point I couldn't see straight. Unbroken sleep swiftly followed.

Friday brunch was a smart-casual affair, and the both of us were grateful we didn't have to suit up or wear ties. Though I eagerly awaited seeing Billy in a suit for the wedding. He looked hot in shorts and a tee, as well as a shirt and jeans, so in a suit, I expected I'd be battling with a semi most of the day. It was a distraction I welcomed.

"You look good." Billy stood behind me as I straightened out my shirt in the reflection of the full-length mirror. A kiss on my neck followed. "You smell fucking edible too."

I laughed, tilting my head to give him better access.

"You just let me know what you need today, and I'm your man, okay?"

Our gazes connected through the mirror. "My man, huh? I like the sound of that."

Billy touched my arm, and I turned eagerly to face him. "Good, and I am, and in all seriousness, you tell me what you need, and I'll make it happen." Intensity shone in his eyes, bringing a wave of warmth through my body like a gentle caress.

"Thank you. And I know I've warned you about my mom, but if she says—"

"Don't worry about me," he said. "I can handle whatever your mom throws at me, all right?"

I smiled despite my heart beating uncomfortably fast. While I'd told him the stories, unless you lived through the wrath of Melissa Crawford, you could never be truly prepared. She was currently campaigning for her second term in office, and while this was a new playing field from when I was a kid, it only meant she was more fierce, more brutal.

Not that she didn't play the part of widow and doting mother to perfection.

I shook off my thoughts of her as much as I could, instead thinking about Mary. The bubble of excitement danced in my gut. Ten years was a heck of a long time. No longer was she an awkward eleven-year-old with braces who was forever in trouble for saying the wrong thing, usually misinterpreting a situation or meaning—something our mom carefully managed, and I expected paid a lot to get stripped out of her somehow.

But from our too brief calls over the years, I knew enough to tell me she was still kind and sweet. There wasn't a trace of viciousness in her. A pang of sorrow for my dad and losing him so early to cancer hit me unexpectedly.

I'd been just eight when he'd passed and had felt

the loss so acutely I'd burrowed deep into myself, spending virtually all of my time helping the nanny with my sister and with my eyes glued to action movies. I suspected that was where my love of running, then my skateboard, and eventually parkour came from. That and the absolute peace and escapism each offered me. Much like an action movie with explosions and over-the-top fight scenes, there was a beautifully addictive numbness in adrenaline.

God, I couldn't wait to get back out there.

"We best head down." Billy picked up his wallet and the room key, placing them in his pockets. Once ready, he reached out for me to take his hand. I did so happily before taking a deep breath and hoping I survived the day.

CHAPTER THIRTEEN

BILLY

FAKE, FALSE, PRETENTIOUS.

Whatever word I assigned to well over half of the people around me, I knew for a fact that Lawrence hadn't exaggerated about anything.

But Mary more than made up for the strangers I greeted with a tight smile.

After just fifteen minutes with her, I was left awestruck by how she maintained the glow of sunshine and positivity when surrounded by such assholes.

Lawrence had managed twenty minutes in a quiet room hugging and catching up with his sister, while I chatted and smiled with Harry, her fiancé, before we'd all been pulled away. In that time, Lawrence's emotions hit me hard. His adoration for his sister was palpable.

And with so many years on the force, my ability to judge character was pretty spot on, and genuine relief filled me when Harry gazed at Mary with nothing but reverence. That they'd found each other in this cesspit of people was a miracle.

But now, standing in the gardens, the tranquil space was marred by the forced conversations and the tension that thrummed through me anytime Melissa Crawford spoke to her son.

Their reunion had been odd.

A large fake smile from the meticulously presented woman and over-the-top greeting, a careful nod from Lawrence, and assessing eyes on me. The whole time, Lawrence's face remained stoic, much like my own. Discomfort rolled off him in waves as he held polite conversation with family and his mom's other guests, skillfully led conversation away from his past, and fielded questions expertly.

Despite being out of the game for ten years, Lawrence was scarily a natural. His ability to act and play the part put a whole new perspective on the man I knew. The whole time, my sadness and frustration mingled with my respect for the guy. And I finally understood his earlier words about the blessing of getting out.

The difficulties he'd faced made him the kind, resilient man he was.

I was sure to God I'd found my new hero. I grinned at the thought.

"What's that smile for?" Lawrence asked, leaning close so his quiet words were just for me.

"Just got a bit of hero worship going on for you right now." My gaze caught his, and even though my tone held humor, I poured the truth of my words into our eye contact.

His smile was sweet, and I loved that he had the confidence to dot a kiss on my neck. When he pulled away, there was a new gleam in his eyes. "You know, talking about heroes, we've never had the very real discussion of superpowers. What would yours be?"

"Ha. Too easy. Strength. But if I could have a particular character's, it would be Superman's for sure. It's a no-brainer."

Lawrence opened his mouth to speak but cut off at the appearance of Governor Crawford.

"There you are, Lawrence. The photographer is with your sister, and she's requested you, dear." She indicated to another part of the garden where Mary was laughing at something her fiancé was saying to her.

Lawrence pursed his lips when he nodded in acknowledgment to his mother. "Sorry," he directed to me. "It shouldn't take long." He reached for my hand.

"I'm sure your friend won't want to watch tedious photographs, Lawrence. I see Chief Bridges, who I'm sure you'd love to meet, Mr. Hilton." I really wouldn't, but I didn't want to make a scene. "Come, come, Lawrence, your sister is waiting." As if on cue, Mary called out.

Lawrence looked at me, his eyes concerned. "You can come with me."

I grinned, loving that he was not being railroaded.

Melissa sighed. "Your friend will—"

"My boyfriend can do as he pleases." A steely gaze was directed toward his mom, one I'd never seen from Lawrence before. It was all levels of hot.

My grin stretched even wider and I stepped into his space, dotting a light kiss on his mouth. "Your boyfriend is all good. If you want me there, I can come."

He shook his head, gaze latching on to mine. "I think you'll be bored to tears. Speaking to Chief Bridges may stop you from drifting off."

I wasn't sure about that, but I simply nodded, saying, "I'll be here when you're done."

"Okay. And don't worry about Bridges. From what I remember of him, he's one of the good ones." He then focused on his mother, whose impatience was carefully masked, but the signs were there if you were good at reading tells. And I definitely was.

I walked beside Governor Crawford, half expecting her to take the time to have a dig, say something about her son and me. She surprised me when she remained silent, only speaking when she introduced me to the chief of police, giving a brief rundown of my history serving.

Someone had clearly done her homework, and she undeniably aced being an impressive hostess.

I shook the chief's outstretched hand. "Good to meet you, sir."

"You too, son." Gray-haired and with clear blue eyes, Chief Bridges struck an impressive figure. He was the same height as me, broad-shouldered, and had deep creasing around his eyes, I imagined from a combination of the stress of the job and smiling—as those laughter lines were definitely there. The smile he sent my way was genuine.

"How are you surviving in the shark pool?" he asked, a twinkle in his eyes.

His question took me by surprise, pulling laughter from me. "I'm coping just fine, thank you, sir." I indicated the mimosa in my hand. "It's much earlier than usual for me, but a couple of these have helped." I flicked a quick look in Lawrence's direction, spotting him with a man maybe a couple of years older. They were talking, and not a single photograph was being taken. I flipped my gaze away, giving Chief Bridges my attention.

He smiled. "I'm envious. I have a meeting this afternoon, or else I would have snuck in a couple myself." His eyes were assessing when he asked, "So Chicago isn't too far away. How'd you manage to get an invite to this affair?"

There was always a moment, the one before me outing myself for the millionth time, that I was curious about reactions. But that curiosity was always at loggerheads with me not giving a shit about anyone's opinion either way. But still, I'd always calculated, needed to know whether this was the time I'd defend myself, walk away, or carry on as easily as if we were talking about the weather.

"I'm here with Lawrence Crawford," I said, my eyes searching out Lawrence again. He was still with the brown-haired man. The guy was smiling widely at my boyfriend, standing a little too close for my liking.

Lawrence didn't seem concerned, though, so I swallowed back my unease. Once again, I returned my attention to the chief.

I had no doubt when I'd looked away, he'd studied me, probably my reaction too. He tilted his head, I expected filing whatever information he drew from that away. "It's been a long time since he came home," he finally said.

At his words, I couldn't help but wonder if he knew what Lawrence's mother had done.

"I imagine Mary is delighted he could make it. She's the sweetest of girls," he continued.

I bobbed my head. "Even after just a few minutes with her, I absolutely agree. Lawrence is happy to see her."

"I can imagine. They were close growing up. From the moment that girl could walk, she was his shadow." He smiled as if lost in memory.

"You've known Lawrence all his life?"

"When he was really young, when Lionel, his dad, was still alive. His death was such a blow to everyone who knew him. He was a good man." Chief Bridges shook his head, sadness shrouding him like a blanket. "And how do you know Lawrence?" he asked, changing the subject and brushing off any lingering sorrow.

I read only genuine curiosity rather than challenge, and answered honestly, "He's been my tenant for well over a year, and now I can add boyfriend to that list."

The chief's brows rose just a little, the only hint of a reaction he gave. "I imagine that smile I've seen on him is as much to do with you as it is seeing his sister." His own eyes flicked over in the direction of Lawrence. I watched him for a beat before following his line of vision.

The governor was now with Lawrence and the man I didn't know. A broad smile sat on her lips as she reached out and touched the tall man's forearm, laughing before saying something to her son, clearly pulling him into the conversation.

Ignoring my unease at the interaction, I answered, "I like to think so," looking at the chief of police, who thankfully appeared to be a decent human being. "He makes me just as happy."

"That's good to hear. I just hope now that he's visited once, he won't be a stranger to his sister." An injection of warmth filled his voice.

But what was more telling was not once had he mention the governor and how she must have missed him. And since he'd noticed Lawrence's happiness, I couldn't help but think he must have known Lawrence and I were together since the moment we arrived, hands firmly linked.

"It all depends on how welcoming everyone is, I expect," I hedged, becoming more convinced the chief wasn't as in the dark as he wished for me to believe. Or maybe that's why I was able to deduce as much. Perhaps he'd made those slips deliberately, but from his reaction to me and Lawrence, there seemed no animosity from him.

His lips curled up at my response, that twinkle back in his eyes. "I expect the man Lawrence has become won't let a thing like that stop him. Families can be pains in the ass at the best of times. When my granddaughter first brought her now-wife home to visit the family," he said pointedly, and my brows lifted in surprise, quickly morphing into appreciation that he'd offered me the detail, "you would have thought it was the start of Armageddon or something, according to one of her uncles." He shook his head, amusement and distaste at the memory seeming to be at war. "I think we all learn how to cull the bad to make room for all the good in the world. It's the only way."

"I couldn't agree more." My mind was blown. From the moment we'd agreed to attend the wedding, both my and Lawrence's guards had been firmly up. Lawrence's wariness about his mother was understandable for sure. And for me, while I liked to give people the benefit of the doubt, I struggled where the governor was concerned.

It would be a hell of a relief for this weekend to go off without a hitch, for the two of us to relax and find genuine happiness in the celebration. But suspicion was second nature to me, so I didn't know how possible that was.

The chief's words provided the tiniest rays of hope, breaking through my tension.

He patted me on the arm. "Just don't buy into the bullshit, son, and you'll both be fine." He shook my hand, saying, "And now might be a good time to interrupt whatever's going on over there with young Lawrence." He said his goodbye, leaving me staring after him and trying to figure out how to unwind enough so Lawrence could have the best of weekends.

But first, I needed to intercept whatever plan the governor was concocting. The man standing so close to Lawrence was good-looking for sure, and I had an uneasy feeling that Governor Crawford hoped Lawrence would do more than appreciate the man's good looks.

WE'D ENDURED BRUNCH, DECLINED THE OFFER TO return to the governor's house for the evening, and came away feeling more positive than when the day had begun. Not only that, I'd stepped in at what I thought was the right moment when Cody, the good-looking guy talking animatedly to Lawrence, had suggested he and my boyfriend meet up for brunch on Sunday morning.

Obviously that was not going to happen. And thankfully, just as I'd overheard Lawrence declining him, Cody had been pulled away by an older man— just in the nick of time before I went into caveman mode.

Lawrence had been left bemused by the whole meeting and offer of a date, which made me feel somewhat better. But it had left me edgy and planted to Lawrence's side the rest of the afternoon.

Plus, because of course there was more, there was the bombshell Mary had dropped. She'd asked Lawrence to give her away.

His emotion had been immediate, rushing to the surface, his eyes shining with pride.

We'd spent two hours with the tailor Lawrence's mom had directed us to. He somehow managed to pull off the slightest of changes on the suit they had on standby, and we walked away with the promise of the delivery of the suit to our hotel by 9:00 a.m. tomorrow morning.

The low hum of tension that had kept me going all day unraveled as I sat in the bath, Lawrence between my legs, leaning against me.

"I'm so tired," he mumbled.

I pressed a kiss to his head. "I bet. I've been wired all day, so Christ knows how you feel."

"Expecting something to happen?"

I snorted with more humor than I expected. "Yeah. That obvious, huh?" I didn't even bother mentioning Cody and my suspicions I had about his mom.

Lawrence shifted his head so he could catch my gaze. "A little, but I felt the same. The high of being with Mary and seeing how happy she is combined with the almighty tension whenever I was a few feet from my mom…." He shook his head. "It wore me out."

"And how are you feeling now other than needing sleep?"

"Wired like you." He settled back more comfortably against my chest and trailed his fingers up and down my thigh. "I'm looking forward to the flight home already. You think that's shitty of me?"

"Hell no. That you came was huge enough. Your mom's lucky you love your sister so much that you were willing to do so."

"She hasn't mentioned a single thing about me being away. Hasn't asked me a single question." Sadness colored his words, though the edge of bitterness added an extra tone. He shook his head. "I'm pissed off that I'm disappointed. Not sure what I was expecting. An acknowledgment maybe. Perhaps a hint of interest, but she hasn't changed."

I trailed my fingers through his hair, trying to soothe him, offer what comfort I could. The movement was hypnotic, helping to quench my bubbling anger at his mom. We remained quiet for some time, resting in the comfort of companionable silence and already considering a bathroom refit with a tub just like this.

It was peaceful and what I was sure we both needed. And in the opulent bathroom, it was easy to pretend this was simply the first of what I hoped to be many romantic breaks away for us.

The thought had me smiling. "You know, when we get dogs, romantic weekend breaks will be a bit trickier."

I didn't need to see Lawrence's face to know he smiled. The soft breaths, the slight relaxation of his shoulders, and the content sigh told me everything.

"It's a good thing we love the outdoors and live close to so many beautiful camping spots."

I grinned. "Maybe we need to go tent shopping at some point. Autumn's always a good time for camping. Cool enough for a fire—"

"And making s'mores."

"—and for us to need to share a sleeping bag."

Lawrence's chuckle had me dotting another kiss to his head.

"Perhaps we need to check out camping before dogs," he said quietly.

A sliver of disappointment trickled its way inside me at his words. I sighed, though, understanding that I was racing toward some sort of invisible goal. "Are you being the adult here?" I asked, forcing lightness into my voice. I wanted it all with him, and I absolutely would be telling him as much, but not here and now. Not when his nerves were as threadbare as they were with the high emotions of this weekend.

He shrugged, and I noticed he kept his gaze firmly on his fingers that were still stroking my thigh. "Is that what I'm doing? I thought I was suggesting the two of us go camping." The words were a little too measured and careful, lightness even more forced than my own.

"Lawrence, turn around so I can see your face." His shoulders slumped, and I added, "Please," before he moved to face me, water sloshing and splashing over the edge of the tub. "What's wrong?"

He looked at me long and hard, and I knew right then he was debating telling me the truth or not. The knowledge hit me in the gut. It didn't matter we'd known each other for well over a year. The reality was it had been just a couple of months that we'd truly got to know each other. And while for me, that was enough time to trust him and believe in us, I had time and experience on my side. Both that were unique to me.

His experiences were very different.

I waited him out, biting back my request for him to open up and share. Tell me what was worrying him so damn much to put that doubt I saw flickering in his beautiful eyes.

"Nothing's wrong," he said, his gaze connecting with mine before settling on his hand that moved to my knee and drew circles there. "It's getting cold. Time to get out." He threw me a smile, but the strain was there, obvious in the dullness in his eyes.

I swallowed back my frustration, my desire to call bullshit. But he was on edge, his emotions fried, that much I was certain of. "Yeah, I'm starting to prune," I offered, aiming for a carefree tone.

The atmosphere had shifted, and for the first time, I felt the tepid water too.

Pushing aside my emotions, I focused on getting

dried and trying not to show how Lawrence's brush-off hurt.

I went straight to the bar, pulled out a beer, and removed the cap. Lawrence was watching. "You want one?" I asked.

"No, thanks. You good if I put the TV on?"

"Sure."

Eggshells were funny things. Sharp and tedious. Uncomfortable.

I closed my eyes once I settled in front of the large windows looking over the city, controlled my breathing. When I opened my lids, I stared out at the skyline, focused on the sparkling lights. The world was a mass of color, and just in the distance, darkness. I smiled when the light split to blackness, reaching out to more rural parts.

"You want to watch this with me?" Lawrence's tentative voice had me turning, my stomach constricting. Not liking the tone, how he was feeling this tension as much as I was, I gave myself an internal shake.

"Absolutely," I said, smiling over at Lawrence. Shirtless and sheet pulled up to his waist in bed, he looked handsome. My smile turned salacious. "Especially when you look so gorgeous."

The slight sag of his shoulders reflected his relief.

My words had been genuine, and I hoped he'd heard that.

"That spot right there has my name written all over it." I indicated the empty side of the bed.

He laughed and tugged back the sheets to his right, patting it. "Then get your ass over here already."

I did so immediately, relieved we could do this: move on for the moment. Words would be needed at some point, but for now, I happily snuggled up with Lawrence on the big bed, watching an old action movie.

There was time for talk of dogs and tents when we got back home.

CHAPTER FOURTEEN

I ducked my head in through the bathroom doorway to say goodbye to Billy. We'd already kissed goodbye, but knowing he was naked and sudsy was too difficult to ignore.

"Get going. Your car will be waiting." He laughed, shooing me out.

With my eyes glued to his bare ass, I sighed loudly. "I'm sure they won't mind waiting five minutes."

Billy snorted and threw me an amused look, his eyebrow cocked. "Five minutes sounds tempting. Perhaps you should've upsold it a bit."

I made to enter the room, about to tell him that with my mouth on him, he'd only need four until I blew his mind.

His "No, get your ass outta here" stopped me in my tracks.

My sigh this time was more petulant and over the top. Yesterday had been exhausting, but a surprisingly okay day, despite the awkward invite I'd received for a brunch date. Part of the day being not as bad as I'd expected was due to spending time with Mary, but the rest was completely due to the man who looked too good to walk away from.

"I wish you were coming with me," I grumbled, knowing full well it would have been completely selfish of me to drag Billy with me. The wedding didn't start for another three hours, but apparently, since I was giving Mary away, I had to be there ridiculously early.

Billy, the hero he was, had offered to tag along, but after yesterday, I'd been feeling braver and more certain about everything. But since then, I'd had a minor flip-out about fucking dogs of all things, and I'd be in forced proximity to my mother without the buffer of two hundred guests, at least until the wedding started.

"I can jump out—"

"No." I huffed out a breath, willing myself to stop being so ludicrous. "I'm okay. I'll see you in just over two hours, right?"

"Absolutely."

"And you'll find me first? Send me a text so I can see you before the ceremony?"

Billy opened the shower cubicle door, a small smile on his face. "Get over here."

I did so eagerly, aware I was being needy but not giving a damn at this point. My nerves were too fried for any embarrassment.

He leaned out, indicating for me to kiss him. As soon as our mouths connected, I relaxed, eased into the touch, and welcomed the calm I took from Billy. When he angled back, his gaze roamed my face. Compassion peered at me from the depths of his eyes.

"You'll be fine, and I'll see you soon, fully dressed and looking dashing in my suit."

I laughed at his words. "Dashing, huh?"

"You better believe it," he said.

"Oh, I do. I have no doubt about it at all."

"Good, now ass outta here."

I pressed my lips to his once more, then left, not wanting to piss off the driver who was waiting for me or my mother, who would no doubt complain about me being five minutes behind schedule.

Once I exited the elevator, I headed toward the main doors. The doorman greeted me. "Your car's ready, Mr. Crawford."

I offered the middle-aged man a smile, saying, "Thanks," and stepped out into the morning sunshine. My gaze traveled immediately to a black Mercedes. The door opened and I faltered. Mario. Unbelievable.

Face stoic, I continued forward.

"Morning, Mr. Crawford."

I tensed my jaw, holding back the jibe and the question on my tongue. I'd be with him for no longer than five minutes, if that. In that time, I'd find the will to keep a lid on my emotions. My nod was sharp in greeting when I sat in the back seat, Mario closing the door behind me.

The five-minute drive felt like an hour. Tension poured off me, a tsunami of frustration that my mom would send Mario. Aware we were about a minute out from our destination, my question fell out, unable to be contained any longer, "Why did my mom send you and not someone else?"

Mario's dark brown eyes connected with my gaze through the rearview mirror. "I'm the main driver now." While it had been ten years, the tone remained the same. He was embarrassed, and rightly so.

"But not the only driver?" I asked. "What happened to Malcolm?"

"He retired two years ago. There's another guy who helps out every now and then, but…."

"But what?" I asked, my frustration clear when he trailed off.

"I offered." His eyes were once more on the road. "I needed to say I'm sorry."

I ground my back molars together. Not having the emotional capacity to deal with Mario and his betrayal or his apology, I simply looked away and out the window. "I don't have it in me today to be forgiving," I finally said, giving him honesty.

I wasn't a fool. Ten years ago, Mario's position had been precarious. He'd been backed into a corner. With the naïve mind of a seventeen-year-old, I'd simply felt betrayed and heartbroken. Today, I accepted more easily the impossible position he'd been in, but that didn't negate the fact I'd lost everything.

But I knew that Mario had become the perfect scapegoat for my mother. The pawn she'd been able to manipulate and use as a reason to finally get me out of the state so she wouldn't need to apologize for me or keep me locked away somewhere.

If it hadn't been Mario, it could have been another guy who I'd finally felt the courage to be with. The double whammy that my young heart had been convinced we loved each other had been hard to take.

I now knew better. I'd been infatuated, for sure. But love?

I glanced at Mario, some of my anger dissipating. My love had been that of a kid feeling the rush of being bold for the first time. I'd never truly loved him. The image of Billy appeared in my mind, the warmth that came with it welcoming and comforting.

Mario pulled up outside the hotel. He didn't angle around to look at me as he spoke, his eyes elsewhere. "I really am sorry. What I did was unforgivable, so I don't deserve your forgiveness. I just needed to let you know I'm sorry. Regardless of everything that happened, you were a kid. I took advantage of that."

His gaze found the mirror again, where my focus was. "Perhaps," I said, then sighed, hating that I felt the need to say more. "But there was nothing forced about anything we did," I clarified. He was an asshole, but I had pursued him, though he'd willingly accepted the two of us being together. "I wanted you."

"And I wanted you," he said, his voice quiet.

Surprise jilted me, kick-starting my heart before it calmed into a steady beat. Knowing what we'd shared wasn't just one-sided eased something deep inside me, a tension that had been balled up in my gut.

Without words, I offered him a small nod and exited the car, not looking back.

From the moment I set foot inside the Madison Concourse, the tone was set. My mom's tight-lipped smiles when she barked orders to everyone around her grated on me, and when she all but pushed Cody—the guy I'd turned down yesterday—in my direction, instructing sweetly that of course, I would assist in doing a walkaround of the reception room checking in on everything, I was close to losing my shit.

Cody had smiled, offering his services with a courtesy that my mom didn't deserve while I'd simply led him away and walked around the room. "I'm sure the planner is on top of everything, and I don't know what exactly I'm looking for." Politeness forced me to speak. But I kept my eyes ahead and clear distance between us.

"I imagine if we tried to offer a single suggestion or touched anything, we'd be in trouble. Kind of makes me want to shift that salt and pepper set an inch to the right."

The humor in his voice had me turning toward him. His amusement was clear and brought a smile to my face.

"If you do that, I'll change the name tags on table fifteen," I said, chuckling.

Cody grinned back. "Done." He looked around us. "Better be quick while the coast is clear."

I didn't know if he was serious or not, but when he went ahead and moved the salt and pepper, throwing me a look of challenge, I stepped up and went to table fifteen.

"If my mom goes on a rampage, I'm pleading complete ignorance," I said, relaxing for the first time since leaving Billy behind this morning.

"Done. Mum's the word." Cody threw me a friendly wink, and I smirked. "You know, when Governor Crawford said she wanted me to meet her son, I had no idea what to expect. I may have hit Google pretty hard." Cody tilted his head, eyes focused and assessing.

I stilled at that. While it was obvious my mom was up to something, considering yesterday and her being pushy with me speaking to Cody, and now this, her intention finally became a little clearer. "Did my mom say why she wanted us to meet?" While I aimed for casual, it was obvious Cody didn't buy it. Too many years had passed for me to play the game and hide my emotions as well as I used to.

A flash of something passed in his eyes, and the slightest flush of heat rose in his cheeks. He cleared his throat. "When your mom knew I was coming alone after a recent breakup, she implied that it was the perfect opportunity for us to meet, and we may have some things in common." He winced. "What I didn't know was that you were dating. Billy, is that your boyfriend's name?"

I nodded, trying to keep my expression neutral. "It is, yeah."

"When I saw you together yesterday after that awkward conversation between us—sorry about that, by the way. The governor can be a difficult woman to say no to—well, it was the first time I saw you relaxed and smiling. You clearly care about him a lot."

The sappy smile that appeared on my face was instant. "I really do. And especially being back here, I've realized more than ever how important he is to me."

Cody nodded. "I'm glad. I know how hard it is to find a good guy. And I know how hard it can be with pushy parents."

I snorted at that. And despite how shitty my mom was for constructing this whole situation, I relaxed, no longer feeling the need to be quite as on guard around Cody. "I think I'm way beyond being bossed around by my mom. A few moments like this, the exception. I'll keep the peace," I admitted, "but I'm heading back tomorrow, and it'll be the end of the charade."

Cody studied my face, his lips pursing as though he was contemplating saying something. "Look," he finally said after a pause. "I'm not—"

"Lawrence, here you are," Deidre, Mom's assistant, said, interrupting Cody. "Governor Crawford is ready for you. It's almost time."

I nodded and turned back to Cody, holding my hand out to the guy. "Good to talk to you."

"You too," he said, shaking my hand.

"Be sure to find me later, and I'll introduce you to Billy," I offered with a smile.

He grinned back. "I'd like that. Good luck today."

I turned and headed back to where I was expected to meet up with Mary, my head spinning a little. Mom attempting to set me up was as frustrating as it was unsurprising. But what added fuel to how pissed I was lay in the fact that the moment I'd RSVP'd, Billy's name was included.

Using me for political matchmaking made my stomach constrict in distaste. Cody's family were investors and bankers, his father the VP of a multimillion-dollar company—all which I'd found out yesterday. I could easily imagine the scenario when my mother found out he was gay and single. I expected it was the real deciding factor in her granting Mary her wish for me to be included in the wedding.

I unclenched my jaw before I opened the door to the suite the bridal party was gathered in. Today was about Mary. It was her day, and I wouldn't let my mom work me up enough that I screwed it up for my sister.

Mary looked beautiful. Complete with fabric that seemed super soft and a style that complimented her shape well, she truly was the picture of beauty. Sadness warred with my pride for her. I'd missed out on so much time with her. She appeared so young, so damn happy, the emotion was all but radiating off her.

"How'd you get so grown up?" I said, walking toward her, relieved she was by herself in the large bedroom. I blocked out the noise from the main area of the suite where a bunch of people were congregating, wanting this moment with Mary.

She turned to me, her eyes bright, her cheeks flushed.

"You're beautiful." I reached out for her hand and she took it quickly and squeezed.

"I can't believe you're really here," she whispered, tears springing in her eyes. My own eyes widened in panic. It would be easy to react the same, be overwhelmed by the riot of emotion unfurling inside me.

I swallowed hard. "I'm so pleased you talked Mom into letting me come."

Confusion flashed in her eyes. "Not sure Mom can be talked into anything. I begged her to let me reach out to you when I first got engaged, but you'd have thought I'd kicked her puppy or something." She shook her head. "She told me a few weeks ago that she'd made it happen—you coming."

Frowning, I mulled over her words, what Mario had said, and what I'd learned about Cody.

"What's wrong?" Mary stepped closer, reaching out and gripping my forearm.

"Nothing," I said quickly, smoothing out the crease between my brows. "I'm just glad I'm here for you." Trying to reassure her, I placed my hand on hers.

"Laurie—"

I smiled at the nickname and shook my head. "Seriously, everything's fine. Plus those tears that would have gotten us both in trouble have disappeared." I grinned, hoping it didn't come across too forced. "I am the master of distraction."

She hesitated until I relaxed my smile. "Truly. You're gorgeous. Your fiancé is a lucky guy, and don't worry, I've already had the talk with him. Threatened to kick his ass if he doesn't treat you right."

I laughed when her eyes bugged, and she smacked me on the arm, saying, "You didn't?"

With my brows waggling up and down, I crossed my eyes, something I always did as a kid to make her laugh.

"Laurie," she said, her voice taking on a whining tone I remembered well.

"It's fine. I didn't really, but Billy was the one who spent time with him yesterday more than me."

A smile softened on his lips. "He's pretty dreamy for an old guy."

"Hey," I said, my laughter joining hers as I tickled her gently at the waist. "He's only a little older than me."

Mary raised her brows high at my response, the "yeah right" very clear in her face.

"Okay," I said with a sigh, "maybe just over ten years. But I'm mature for my age." And I seriously was. Being on my own for so long had forced me to grow up fast. I kept my smile in place though, not letting the hurt of my past show.

"Mature," she said with a snort that made me chuckle. "Hardly. I know it's been a while since I saw you in the flesh, but you're still the big brother who used to leave 'gifts' aimed to make me scream in my bed." Her laughter died off, focus intense when she then said, "Billy seems like a great guy. Obviously he must be for you to love each other so much."

I opened my mouth to refute her words but was interrupted by the door opening.

"Okay, it's time for the veil, and we're ready," the planner, Violet, said.

Mary nodded, and I placed a gentle kiss on her cheek before getting out of the way.

While waiting, I pulled out my phone. There were no missed calls. Since it was already on silent, I'd been checking off and on for the past half hour or so, waiting for news from Billy, but still nothing. It was odd, but with how manic it was, I probably wouldn't get the chance to see him properly anyway.

I sent him a text, and waited a beat, willing an immediate response. None came so I quickly hit dial only for it to ring out.

Looking away from my phone, I spotted my mom talking quietly to her assistant. I headed over, forcing my feet in the direction, wishing I didn't have to, but since she planned the event, she was the person to ask. Once I was before them, Mom moved her gaze away from her assistant and to me.

Before she spoke, she returned a final look at Deidre, saying, "Just get it done." The words hit their mark as the harassed assistant hightailed out of the suite. "What can I do for you, Lawrence? We're almost ready to begin."

My eyes connected with hers. I refused to let her impatience and sharp question unsettle me. "Billy was supposed to be here and let me know when he arrived. Have you seen him?"

With pursed lips, she gave the barest of head shakes when she said, "No."

I frowned. "Are you—"

"Lawrence," she said, cutting me off, exasperation evident, "if he were here, I'm sure you would have seen him by now. Perhaps he's running late."

There was no chance of that. I pulled my phone out of my pocket. "I'll just call—"

She all but snatched the cell out of my hands. "This needs to be off. You're about to walk your sister down the aisle. Your focus should be on her and not showing her up on her big day." Sneering, she shook her head. "And if that *friend* of yours can't be bothered to show up, perhaps he's finally worked out you can do better than him."

Anger sent heat to my face. "What the hell have you done?" It was my turn to sneer.

When she tutted at me, it was only the sound of my sister's voice that stopped me from exploding. "Really, Lawrence, now's not the time. Stop being so selfish and go and support your sister."

Apparently, we were done.

She walked off, leaving the heavy scent of her sickly perfume behind, and me with shaking hands. I just had to hope like hell that Billy was okay and that he was already seated, and I'd spot him when walking Mary down the aisle.

For a fleeting second, I thought back to me freaking out on him yesterday. And while he hadn't challenged me, he'd been hurt. I shook my head. My freak-out during the discussion about dogs was insignificant and now left me cringing. It was me—fresh with the hurt of being abandoned by my family—who'd been slammed with the reminder that Billy could do the same.

Getting attached and opening myself up to him was the hardest thing I'd ever done in my life. The fear of me being in reach of everything I ever dreamed of, to then have it ripped away from me was more than I would be able to handle.

I exhaled deeply, calming myself.

This situation wasn't about that.

Billy not being here was all about Mom and whatever twisted shit she'd got into. The certainty of that thought flitted through me, forcing clarity to my brain.

And while whatever Mom had done could possibly be the final nail that pushed Billy away, I refused to believe that.

Billy was protective and thoughtful. He'd also made me a promise to be here for me.

I forced a smile when Mary reached me, my mind still on Billy. I had to believe I'd see him in all his suited hotness in a matter of minutes when I walked my sister down the aisle. My mission would be to not stumble and trip on my tongue as I did so.

CHAPTER FIFTEEN

BILLY

Fury was not something to laugh at. But if I didn't do exactly that, it was possible I would lose my shit completely and get myself arrested. That would have been the icing on the clusterfuck of a cake.

"Get your supervisor." I shook my head, my almost maniacal laughter dying down and turning into a humorless laugh. I was tired of making the same demands, but with no other choice than to keep trying, I stood my ground.

The security guy before me didn't look impressed at my demand, but he could take a running leap. In fact, I'd give him the head start of a push if he continued to scowl at me.

"It's simple. You're not on the list, which means you don't gain entry."

My head shake was slow and short. "And you're not listening to me. Get your supervisor down here, someone with a bit of common sense and who I hope to God isn't just some beefed-up thug playing at being a cop."

Said beefed-up thug apparently didn't like that one bit. His eyes narrowed and he leaned into my space. "You need to leave."

I held his stare, hands fisting, my breaths shallowing. "Don't get too comfortable, asshole," I finally said, stepping away. It was too dangerous to stay in front of the dick. Years had passed by since I'd been in any sort of scuffle, and doing it now, outside where a wedding was due to— I looked at my wristwatch. Shit, any second now it would be starting.

It was clear I wasn't getting in, and having left my phone in the hotel by mistake meant I couldn't give Lawrence any warning. I shook my head from the second wind of anger threatening to rise in me. The whole point of me being here was to support Lawrence and help him get through this weekend, survive the governor and the piranhas in her midst.

And I couldn't even do that.

Hopelessness was a familiar emotion. After losing Clark, my ineptitude had ridden me hard. It had taken many hours of counseling to accept his death had been out of my control, as well as dealing with my guilt. My depression had hit me something fierce, one of the symptoms of my PTSD, and I'd be damned if the governor would lead me down that path again.

There was no doubt in my mind that this was all her. How couldn't it be?

What I wanted to know was what her end game was. Regardless of what she hoped to achieve, I wouldn't let her insert herself between Lawrence and me. If Lawrence wanted her back in his life, I'd deal with that, but from all I knew of her and Lawrence, I couldn't imagine that happening in the foreseeable future. Especially not after this stunt.

With it obvious that I couldn't do anything about getting in at the moment without causing chaos and most likely resulting in my arrest, I headed back to our hotel to grab my phone. My call to Lawrence would have to wait, since he was likely leading Mary down the aisle at this second. But I'd send him a text so the first time he could check, he'd know this was completely out of my control.

ME: I'M HERE. OUTSIDE. I'M SORRY. SECURITY wouldn't let me in. My name was no longer on the list. I'll wait outside the hotel for you.

I'd considered staying in our room, and even contemplated propping up the bar, but as pissed off as I was, I needed to be there for Lawrence.

While him finding out what had happened would make his stressful day a shitty one, my selfish need to let him know this wasn't on me drove me forward; that and my protective instincts.

I leaned against the small wall directly across the road, opposite the entrance to the large brick building. The security remained on the door and spotted around, and truth be told, I was surprised no one had come and asked me to move on or had called the cops on me yet.

I'd been waiting for thirty minutes, so I hoped anytime soon my cell would be ringing or Lawrence would appear at the door. Seeing movement, I looked up. Recognition immediately registered, and I pushed off from the wall.

Smiling, I crossed the road, eyes on the security guard, who immediately straightened, hand moving to his belt. At the shift, Chief Bridges peered over his shoulder. His eyes widened in surprise before he turned.

"Billy Hilton." He extended his hand to me, which I took, casting a quick glance at the guard to his right, hoping he was listening to every word. I just prayed this played out as I hoped.

"Chief Bridges, good to see you." I released his hand.

"And you. Nice ceremony." He nodded. "Not as long-winded as some of the ones I've attended recently, which was a heck of a relief." His amused smile was joined by a wink.

"Unfortunately, I wouldn't know."

A frown creased the space between his brows. "What do you mean? You didn't attend?"

I shook my head, my frustration flaring anew. "Afraid not. When I arrived this morning, my name was no longer on the list, and the… *gentleman* here refused to investigate further or reach out to Lawrence for me." The flare sparked and grew just thinking about Lawrence and how he must be feeling, what he must be thinking.

The chief's brows dipped even lower. "Is that so?" Before I could answer, he turned to the man on duty. "Who's in charge of the list?"

"The governor and her personal detail oversee it."

The chief nodded. "And were changes made this morning?"

The guard hesitated, which told us both everything we needed to know. "We were provided with a new list this morning. I'm unsure if there were changes on there."

"Right." Chief Bridges turned to me. "Come on. Let's get you inside."

"Sir, we can't let him in without—"

The chief's shoulders turned to stone, and in a voice that would have had me shitting myself if it were directed at me, he said, "Need I remind you I've been directly involved with every aspect of today's security plan, and that my men and women are as involved as the private team?"

The man on duty wasn't a cop, but there was no doubt he knew exactly who the chief was and the power he wielded.

"Are you going to step aside, or are you going to continue wasting my time?" Chief Bridges' voice was even, controlled.

Sensibly, the security guard stepped out of the way, eyes averted. I held my sneer back, knowing he'd just been doing his job, but he was still an asshole.

Once inside, I exhaled. "Thanks for your help, sir."

He nodded and patted me on the back. "Just keep your wits about you, okay, son?"

I nodded and shook his hand. "Will do."

"Billy." Lawrence's voice had me turning. His eyes were wide, his face flushed, and relief evident when he said, "Thank Christ."

"And that's my cue," the chief said, taking his leave back toward the main door after patting Lawrence on the shoulder. But Lawrence's focus was completely on me.

As soon as the chief was gone, Lawrence was in my space, one hand on my forearm, the other wrapping around me and pulling me close. A tremor worked its way through his body, hitting me hard and raising my guilt that I'd allowed this to happen.

"I'm so sorry I wasn't here for the service. I tried." He pulled away as I spoke, his gaze filled with some sort of emotion he was battling with. "I should have just come with you this morning and then this—"

"No," he said, interrupting me. "This isn't your fault."

I exhaled in relief, not realizing how much it meant that he understood without question.

"My mother took your name off the list?"

"I believe so, yeah. It was lucky Chief Bridges spotted me and got me in."

Lawrence shook his head and held my hand, squeezing. Intensity shone in his gaze. "I'm so sorry.

That was such a shitty thing for her to do. I should have expected her to do something like this."

With my hand in his, I tugged, drawing him closer. "I'm here now. That's all that matters, right?" There was still so much more to be said and worked out, but now wasn't the time. "Anyway, how was the service? Everything go okay?" The calm in my voice surprised the hell out of me. It hid away the anger still churning inside me. But there'd be time enough to deal with that after.

Lawrence's eyes softened, and my relief intensified that I was handling this the right way.

"It was great. Mary looks gorgeous. She grinned through the whole service. It was kinda sweet."

"Yeah?"

"Definitely. I'm relieved she's found someone, you know? She told me that she's already packed, and her new home is ready for her to move into." He shook his head, nose scrunching. "It's all a bit weird, though, a bit Stepford if you ask me. I know part of Mom's campaign is all about tradition, but that Mary's never lived with her husband...." He scrunched his nose again. "Yeah, not sure I could be so trusting."

I grinned. "You know, we've survived, what, nine weeks now of living together?"

Lawrence's eyes widened at that, but he didn't say anything.

My smile fell. "What's wrong?"

Hesitation bled into his eyes, across his mouth as he gnawed on his lip. "Nothing."

I couldn't keep back my sigh. "Shouldn't I have said that or something?" I made to release his hand, feeling a vulnerability that put me on edge, but he gripped tighter, not allowing me to escape.

"It's not you, honest. It's just… my head is a mess." He swallowed hard and stood straighter, gaze flicking away. "Can we talk about this later?"

The reality of where we were had me nodding. "Yeah, of course." Unease colored my words, and I hated it. This whole day so far had been a disaster.

Lawrence stepped into my space, and he pressed a tender kiss to my lips. "Thank you. And I promise it's not you, okay?"

Reading Lawrence wasn't always the easiest thing for me to do, but I had to have faith in him and us. I bobbed my head, my smile tentative.

"I need to find Mary for my photos," he said, his exhaustion clear as we started walking hand in hand. "Promise you won't leave my side?"

Heat bloomed in my chest. "I'm here if you need me."

"I do." His words had me side-eyeing him. He cast me a quick glance, whether responding to my movement or to see my reaction, I didn't know. But whatever he read on my face caused him to smile.

"Thanks."

He led us on through a corridor and a couple of rooms. Low rumbles of conversation greeted us, and we continued in that direction, entering the large space set up for photos.

"Laurie, there you are. We need you and Billy for the next family shot." Mary's happiness filled every word and showed in every expression that crossed her features.

"We're here, sorry." Lawrence led me further into the room. And despite my leaden feet, I remained by his side.

I scanned the room, my eyes catching the governor's. I sent her a hard stare. While I wouldn't be challenging her here, my good manners could only stretch so far.

The woman's face soured, and a thrill of satisfaction slid through me.

The photographer's assistant ushered us on. I followed, uncertainty quickly finding its way to me.

"Lawrence," I said quietly, "I'm not sure I should be in these photographs." It pained me to speak the truth, but these were Mary's wedding photos, ones she'd always have. Being the man who her brother had been officially dating for three weeks didn't really earn me a place in them.

He turned to me just at the edge of the conversation going on as the assistant got to work with the photographer setting up. "I want you in them. So does Mary."

I huffed out a small breath, unsure whether to push or not. We knew this weekend was going to be stressful and challenging, but my nerves were fried, and I was sure Lawrence's were too. While certain about my feelings for Lawrence, the depth of them, the past twenty-four hours had reminded me how worlds apart we were in many ways. And while I wanted to believe none of that mattered, I couldn't help the hesitation impinging on my actions.

I steeled my nerve. There was no doubt my words were going to piss Lawrence off, but I couldn't not share the concern beating at me. "And you want me in them for you and not to piss your mom off?"

He released his grip on my hand as if he'd been burned. Hurt touched his eyes immediately, and my own guilt rushed forward. His mouth tightened and his wide, hurt-filled eyes narrowed. "Are you serious?" The quiet of his voice held an edge I'd never heard before. And while regret ate at me, I had to ask the question. "You think I brought you all this way for that?" He clenched his jaw.

I wanted to close my eyes, rub my hands over my face, but losing eye contact with him felt wrong. Tension crackled between us. I needed to cut through it, and fast. "No, I don't think that," I said quietly, all too aware we weren't alone. Their mumbled conversation drifted over us. "I just wanted to make sure something as significant as being in a wedding photograph is for the right reasons." I exhaled, but rushed to continue, worried he'd cut me off. "If you want me in there for you, for us, and because you see me in your future, then I'm there by your side." I paused, hating we were doing this here and now. Hating that this shitshow of a day had forced us into this position. And frustrated I was making this a thing.

But I'd been on this earth for too long to ignore the significance.

A slow exhale escaped from the man before me. While hard eyes remained cast my way, his jaw loosened. "It's been three weeks." The words were quiet, with no inflection. I waited, not sure what he meant or how he intended to continue.

"Lawrence, we need you now." His mother's voice cut through us, tearing our gazes away. The tightness in Lawrence's jaw was immediate. "I'm sure Mr. Hilton won't mind waiting to the side for a little while," she continued. "These are family photographs, after all."

He turned back to me. Something had shifted in his eyes. With a softening gaze that made me catch my breath, the small smile that joined it was powerful enough that my heart flipped. "I get it," he said quietly, his words just for me. When he reached out, his hand once more clasping mine, I exhaled, some of my strain releasing.

"It's just a lot of pressure for you in a nightmare situation," I finally clarified. "And that request right there—"

"—validated your concern," he said, cutting me off.

"Yeah, and this is once again not a conversation I wanted us to be having right now." My voice was carefully quiet, reassuring.

He nodded, and my relief matched his as his shoulders sagged a little, his smile sitting a little easier. "I want you at my side in the photos."

The statement was clear, intentional, and hell if my already somersaulting heart didn't warn me to calm my shit down before I had a heart attack.

"All right then. Wherever you want me, I'm there." This time I grinned before pressing my lips quickly to his. It was short, sweet, and seemed to piss off the governor even more. Her huff reached us over the photographer's instructions and the mumbled conversation of the bridal party.

Somehow we made it through the photo shoot and the reception, where I was seated with a group at what was clearly the "losers" table, far away from the head table where Lawrence was.

He'd been pissed as all hell when he'd found out. Me? I'd been expecting it, so took it in stride.

After the speeches, which caused an ache in my chest for the guy who'd missed out on so much time with his sister, I smiled at Lawrence dancing with her. His exhaustion was pronounced, evident in his tired eyes and slight limp. Spending so much time on his feet today would have been a shock to his muscles and his repaired bone. But his happiness as he twirled his sister on the dance floor, impressing the heck out of me, was no doubt just what he needed.

This reunion had been ten years in the making. His sister's exuberance simply made it sweeter.

The whole formality of the event was mindboggling. I'd been to a police ball a time or two, even a couple of more high-end weddings, but this, with security, the rigidity of the day's schedule, was the most bizarre.

One day if I got married, the ceremony would be so far removed from this event. Simple, family and friends, and the sun at my back was my idea of perfect.

"Hey." The deep voice at my side took me by surprise. I jerked my head in that direction to find the same guy who'd spent too much time with Lawrence yesterday at my side. "Name's Cody," he said, hand outstretched.

Unable to ignore the offered hand, I gripped and shook, giving him a head bob. "Billy."

"Yeah, I know. Lawrence said earlier."

My gaze darted over his face, trying to get a read on the man. He was handsome, younger than me, but a little older than Lawrence. His no doubt expensive suit molded his frame, fitting him perfectly, and he carried it off with ease. A man used to wearing fine clothes and definitely suits.

"You spoke to him earlier?" I asked, ensuring my voice was even. Jealousy was a hell of a thing, and despite the swirls of it in my gut, I had to temper it, control it.

"Yeah." He flicked his gaze in the direction of the dance floor, a small smile on his lips, and I knew immediately his focus was on my Lawrence. By the time he looked back at me, my brows were high, a question and challenge obvious in my eyes.

Pink tinted his skin, pissing me off more, knowing my assessment was right. He rubbed at the back of his neck while I kept myself in check, waiting for him to speak.

"The governor," Cody said, his voice the tone of someone conspiring, "she kind of threw us together. Yesterday and today," he clarified.

Sneering would have been a dead giveaway, so instead, I clamped my back molars down hard, my focus on controlling my reaction. That he was here talking to me told me he was either stirring or clarifying the situation. For his sake, I hoped for the latter.

"I told Lawrence as much earlier. He seems like a nice guy and deserved to be told."

I slowly exhaled at his words. "He is a nice guy, the best," I said, my tone no longer filled with ice.

Cody nodded. "The governor approached me earlier, indicating quite forcefully that the next dance would be me and Lawrence."

"You what?" Confusion and frustration swam in my mind. "That's one hell of a statement for a woman who—" I caught myself in time. Lawrence's history was not mine to share. With a shake of my head, I asked, "Is there a reason why you're telling me this?"

A smile lit up Cody's features, transforming his rigid handsomeness into something more. "I have no allegiance to the governor. She may have business and political ties to my father, but not me," he said. His smile dropped when he said, "And the fact that her gay son has not been seen or heard of in the last ten years gives me a lot more insight into the situation."

I let him continue without interruption, more relieved than ever that Lawrence and I were far removed from the impact of his mom.

"I wanted to give you the heads-up and encourage you to cut in as soon as possible." He finished in earnest, a new intensity in his voice I wasn't expecting. "Using Lawrence and me for her latest agenda is not okay," he clarified.

I bobbed my head, reaching out and shaking his hand once more. "Thank you."

"Anytime." The song was drawing to an end, and both of our gazes traveled to the dance floor.

"See you in a few," he said with a wink before making his way to the dance floor where Lawrence stopped and placed a kiss on his sister's cheek, then appeared to whisper something in her ear.

Mary's husband arrived at her side as the next song started. I watched as Lawrence laughed at something and turned. Just before his gaze reached mine, his mom was by his side, indicating to Cody.

That Cody had prepared me was a good thing. My

reaction otherwise could have pushed me that step too far, my possessive nature nudging close to the surface.

When panic flushed across Lawrence's face, obvious even at this distance, I couldn't help the smile that tugged my lips even as I knew I should feel shitty for his discomfort. But damn if his reaction didn't make me happy.

They were hand in hand, Lawrence seeming to listen intently to whatever Cody was saying. In the next moment, his gaze found mine, eyes wide, searching. A small twitch of his lips followed.

And that was my cue.

On the way to the dance floor, I worked hard at ignoring the nudges and stares, the wide eyes and looks of surprise directed Lawrence and Cody's way, though not all were in disapproval or contempt. Which I supposed clarified the governor's goals all along.

That may well be. She could have her show for sure. But no way would it be with another man in Lawrence's arms.

"Mind if I cut in?" I asked, eyes only on Lawrence, whose toothy grin left me smirking.

Cody stepped out of the way, and I looked at him. "By all means." He followed up with a wink.

I offered a chin lift, my hands quickly finding

purchase on Lawrence. "You good to lead?" I asked, already recognizing his dance skills were significantly better than my own.

He laughed, the sound light and doing wonderful things to the dark cloud hanging over us the majority of the day. "I'm happy to," he said, holding me close, gaze remaining connected to mine.

"I missed you at dinner."

A flash of guilt crossed over his face. "I'm so sorry—"

I shook my head, cutting him off. "I didn't say it to guilt you. It is what it is. I just missed spending time with you is all."

His shoulders relaxed a little. "And how was your table?"

I grinned. "An interesting bunch. Painfully quiet to begin with, but Harry's aunt Agnes is hilariously entertaining once she's had three glasses of champagne. She kept up a running commentary of the inner workings of Harry's family and told tales I'm sure they would've preferred to have kept buried."

"I'm jealous. I had Mary, but obviously, she's in 'Mary's married land,' and she wouldn't take her eyes off Harry. I had Mom the other side of me." Lawrence's nose scrunched in distaste. "She was doing a hard sell of Cody most of the time, and still hasn't asked a single question about me, how I'm doing. Nothing." While he gave a shrug, the pinch of his lips showed that it stung.

A pang of gratitude hit me for my own parents. While I wasn't that close with them anymore, which was totally my fault, they were supportive of every decision I'd ever made. Supportive of me sometimes with questions, but always with love.

We continued to move to the rhythm of the music, and I made the most of spending these few moments with him. There hadn't been enough of them today. After a moment of quiet, I asked softly, "Do you regret coming?"

He sighed, leaning in and resting his head on my shoulder. I pulled our held hands close to our chests. While aware this was more like late-night dancing before the lights came on rather than three dances into the evening, I'd do anything to give him the comfort he needed.

"Regret's the wrong word," he eventually said. "I'm happy I was able to be a part of Mary's day, but a shotgun wedding in Vegas would have been awesome." He chuckled, and I joined in, pressing my lips to his temple.

"Are you going to have it out with your mom?" I asked, my voice tentative. This whole situation was not only alien, but it was bullshit. I was forty-three years old and felt caught in a high school drama or some crap.

While I didn't need that in my life, weeks ago my feelings for Lawrence had hit me hard to the point of giving me the wake-up call I needed. I'd put up with the game for him. The whole situation was not him, though, most was out of his control, but I was curious how he would handle it.

Earlier I hadn't been lying to myself when I'd recognized how different we were. A part of that was how we reacted to situations. At the end of the day, despite our differences, despite perhaps our different stages in life, Lawrence was who I wanted. And I did, something fierce.

"I'm tempted to leave tomorrow and not look back," he said, head still pressed against me. "But it's time for me to say my piece and simply deal, you know?"

I nodded, sure he could feel my movement.

"For years she's been the reason I couldn't settle, and I'm not prepared for that to happen anymore."

Pride swelled in my chest. The music cut off just before I was able to speak.

Lawrence pulled away, gaze finding mine. "Thanks for cutting in."

I grinned. "As if I wouldn't." I dotted a gentle kiss on his mouth before indicating for us to move off the dance floor. "Drink?"

"Definitely."

We headed toward the bar but were stopped at the edge of the room, just a few feet from the promise of beer. I inwardly groaned when I peered into the face of the governor. Her eyes were tight, lips pulled together, looking like a monkey's ass.

I willed away the image, terrified I'd snort in laughter.

"What can I do for you, Mom?"

The casual sureness of Lawrence's voice took me by surprise. I glanced his way, taking in his easy smile that belied the hardness I could see in his eyes, even from my position.

When I refocused on his mom, her eyes widened slightly before returning to a more controlled state. It seemed she was surprised by Lawrence too.

"I want a word with you in private."

I pulled my lips between my teeth, body rigid as I waited for Lawrence to respond.

Out of the corner of my eye, I saw him angle his head. "Sure. Just out in the next room?" She bobbed her head and turned, stopping when Lawrence tugged on my hand, saying, "Come on. I promise beer soon."

"Alone." The demand clipped her word short.

"I'm happy for Billy to be there."

"I hardly think it's appropriate for a friend to be joining us for—"

"Billy is more than a friend. We're together. Now, he can come or I'm heading to the bar."

Words caught in my throat. I swallowed them down, unable to interfere. The desire to do just that and tell the governor exactly what I thought of her rode me hard, but it would only end up with me being kicked out and Lawrence being forced into an even more awkward position.

"Fine." Her nostrils flared before she spun on her heel and led the way.

As we followed, I leaned in close. "You okay?"

A stilted head bob was my answer.

Powerlessness was not something I enjoyed. Ever. And when it was in response to someone I cared deeply for, my need to protect and intervene was difficult to ignore.

But from everything I knew about Lawrence, one thing was certain. He didn't need my protection. He'd been coping, surviving… hell, more than that, living in a world for the past ten years with no one at his back.

While he didn't need me to step in and take over, he had my unconditional support.

Once the three of us were in the quiet room to the side of the main party, I remained silent, curious about what she had to say and exactly how she thought this would play out.

The steel in her eyes set the tone, while the venom in her words left me reeling. The whole time, I remained rigid, watching Lawrence carefully, reading him, and ready and hoping for my chance to step in before getting him the hell out of this place.

CHAPTER SIXTEEN

LAWRENCE

"I gave you the opportunity to not make a fool of yourself and humiliate me, but you had to throw that in my face too." Contempt rolled off my mom as she shook her head. "You need to ask your friend to leave before he ruins everything I've been working toward. I will not have you swan in after all of these years and—"

"Swan in?" A sharp laugh slipped past my lips. "I wouldn't be here if you hadn't summoned me with the promise to support Mary."

She barely paused for breath before responding, "You're doing a fine job of supporting your sister by giving everyone a show. You should be ashamed of yourself." Venom dripped off every word. "I'm disgusted with your behavior—"

"My behavior or me?" I asked, not sure if I really wanted to know. But there wasn't a chance I'd take her spouting hatred at me lying down.

Her lips pursed and she didn't respond, which was answer enough for me. A war raged inside me. I didn't know whether to be pissed by her lack of response or celebrate the fact I'd made the woman speechless. Either way, sadness cemented itself in my chest while anger bubbled close to the surface.

Keeping my emotions in check took more than sheer will. I absorbed the warmth from Billy's hand holding mine, the quiet strength of solidarity. Willing myself to calm so I wouldn't reveal my wrecked emotions, I said, "It's obvious a gay son was on your agenda this weekend." Emotion clogged my throat despite my desperation for control. "I can't make it any clearer than letting you know I'm not interested in anything from you or to do with you."

Deep red flooded her face, and she opened her mouth to speak. I shook my head, surprised when that simple gesture cut her off. Perhaps I wasn't reining in my emotions as well as I hoped.

"No. Enough. I'm here for Mary. That's it." I forti-fied my courage, on a roll and no longer able to simply walk away. "When you threw me out ten years ago, it was the best thing that could have ever happened to me."

The red in her face turned crimson. "Don't be so hysterical. I didn't throw—"

"When you threw me out when I was seventeen years old," I said, my voice hard as I cut in, "you broke something in me." I shook my head again, hands trembling. Billy remained my sentinel, boosting my resolve. "Sometimes I don't know how I got through those days." I snorted humorlessly. "Hell, *years* by myself."

"The money was there for you to continue to pay for your education. You can't blame me for not taking it."

"But I do blame you. Why the hell would I take money off someone who hated me so much they threatened and made it explicitly clear they never wanted to see me again? Why would I ever have wanted to achieve anything and have you touch it in any way?"

For the first time, something beyond anger and contempt crossed her features. Her face blanched.

"I didn't mean—"

"Save your breath. I'm not interested in anything you have to say." I glanced to my side, gaze settling on Billy, who turned in my direction. The look in his eyes nearly undid me. Emotion—fierce and strong—bled through their depths.

He didn't smile. He didn't wink. He didn't do anything for a moment other than stare at me with unchecked affection. My gaze moved to his neck when I saw the bob of his Adam's apple.

"I love you." His quiet words were steady, cutting through the heaviness in my heart, making it unstable and freeing the emotion I'd been terrified to release.

My eyes flicked to his—at least one of the emotions now there was much clearer.

Ill-timed laughter bubbled in my throat before springing free. I couldn't help it. Couldn't hold back. My feelings needed to let loose, and between the sorrow and anger at my mom and the depth of my own love for the man who gripped my hand, the only escape was deep laughter that simultaneously lightened my heart while filling it to the brim.

"This is ridicu—"

My laughter cut off at the first syllable from my mom, my own words drowning her out. "I love you too." My grin followed, wide and unrestrained.

"You need to leave if this is how you're going to behave."

Attention back on the woman who I was eager to never see again, I nodded. "Fine by me." My thoughts went to Mary, filling with regret, but she'd be fine. She would barely notice me leaving, happy in her wedding day celebrations. At least with her moving away from our mother, it would mean I'd no longer be restricted from making contact with her.

With my focus on Billy, I said, "We just need to say goodbye to Mary, okay?"

"Yeah, whatever you need."

"I don't think so. I can ask security to escort you out."

Billy's abrupt laughter startled me. Wide-eyed, I looked at him.

"Why don't you go ahead and do that, *Governor*. Perhaps we can see what extra attention we can find along the way."

Stony-faced, my mom stared at him.

Taking her silence as answer, Billy nodded. "Thought so. You know, when I was a cop, it was my absolute belief in justice that got me through my days, helped me wade through the shit needed to keep doing the right thing." A sardonic smirk lifted Billy's lips, something I'd never seen before. The effect was mesmerizing and slightly fucking terrifying. "Now I believe in karma." I swallowed my smile as he spoke, immediately thinking about our past conversations. "Not having a badge means I need to grasp at justice where I can find it. And, Governor Crawford, I have zero doubt you'll get yours one day. And Lawrence will be so far removed from your clutches that he won't give a shit about the misery you find yourself wallowing in."

She jerked at his words, her face turning ashen. "Lawrence, you're my s—"

"No." Resolve steeled Billy's abrupt response. "He's mine. You lost any right you had to him when he was seventeen fucking years old."

Blood roared in my ears, the sound deafening. Alongside the roar was the pounding of my heart. And holy shit. He just said that. I didn't know whether to laugh, swoon, be pissed, or drop to my knees. And from the concern clear in his eyes and dipping his brows, he saw my difficulty too.

"You ready?" he asked, his voice low and just for me.

I blinked, the action slower than usual, but it helped adjust my focus and center myself as I looked at the man gripping my hand. There was so much I wanted to say, some of it making it hard not to hold back the twitch of my lips at his proclamation. But it wasn't the time. I'd already spilled my heart with those three words I'd never said to another man before.

I'd thought they'd be hard to say. Had even debated

saying them for a while, my fear of it being too soon and me being too lame preventing me.

But they'd fallen out easily, perhaps even automatically in reply to his own words. It didn't mean I felt or meant them any less.

"Yeah," I finally said, putting my back to my mother and taking a step toward the door, looking up for the first time. I faltered, my gaze slamming into Cody's and then drifting over and up to an older man's, the face I recognized more from my youth than now. Then he hadn't been the chief of police he was today.

Amusement shot through me, fast and fierce, alongside my choked words, "Shit, Mom, looks like karma's here already."

CHAPTER SEVENTEEN

BILLY

Lawrence slept the whole flight home, and I'd slipped into sleep during the car journey after that, only waking up from the gentle stroke on my cheek. By the time we fell into bed, we'd kissed, snuggled close, and finally passed out.

With the brightness bleeding through my closed eyelids, the steady beat of Lawrence's heart welcomed me as I woke in his arms. We lay in my bed, my face resting against his chest.

After Cody and Chief Bridges bore witness to a fair amount of what went down between Lawrence and Melissa Crawford, followed by my vocal shutdown of the woman, we'd left. We'd said goodbye to Mary, faking our good moods and a digestive problem, and had gotten a promise from her to visit soon with her new husband.

It was on the way out when Cody had caught up with us, asking for both our numbers to check in with us later in the week. We'd had no idea how much he or the chief had heard, but from their darkened looks directed the governor's way when we'd initially passed them by, I expected they'd overheard a fair amount.

I was not in the least bit regretful. And honestly, I was freakin' impressed with myself that I hadn't lost my shit. My possessive streak remained active for sure, but that I'd contained my need to dominate the situation was progress I hadn't expected.

While I had no follow-up appointments with the therapist I'd last seen about six months ago, I was sure she'd be impressed too.

"You awake?" Lawrence's gruff voice cut through my thoughts.

In response, I angled back so I could see his face. "Morning." My voice was equally gruff. Leaning up, I made it clear I wanted his lips on mine. With a tender smile, he did just that.

I moved properly, aware his arm was probably dead, and dropped my head to the pillow next to his. "You sleep all right?" I asked.

Covering his mouth as he yawned, he nodded before answering, "Yeah, like a log. You?"

"Yeah, could have slept through a zombie invasion."

Lawrence grinned. "No chance. I would have woken you up so you could protect me."

I snorted. "One of the many things I've learned about you, Lawrence, is you don't need my protection." How he'd stood up to his mom was impressive as hell. The woman exuded power, and it was clear she rarely encountered the word no. So Lawrence finally laying out his feelings had been a spectacular moment. And I imagined he really needed it to move on.

We'd talked a lot over the past few weeks. I'd put enough together to see just how resilient the man was, and maybe now, he'd finally feel settled.

Lawrence's grin softened, his hand moving to my face where he stroked his fingers over my brow. "You think?"

I nodded. "Definitely."

"Thanks, but I'll take your protection with the zombies. You're the one trained to defend people and use guns, right?"

When he bobbed his brows up and down, I laughed. "In that case, maybe we need to become one of those preppers and start hoarding ammo and stuff."

"Hmm, maybe not to that extreme. I was thinking more of you being my human shield."

I snorted and reached out for him, squeezing his waist and digging my fingers in a little. "Is that right?"

"Maybe," he said, laughing. The sound wrapped around me, relaxing me in a way I loved. His carefree laugh was quickly becoming one of my favorite sounds. When his laughter died off, he asked, "What time you working today?"

"I told Jacob I'd be there at ten. Molly has to be at the vet clinic for eleven thirty, so it'll give me some time to check everything's okay before driving him over. After that, I'm heading to Austin's for a couple of hours." I glanced at the time, seeing it was seven thirty. "What time are you at work?"

"Noon. I'm there for the lunch rush. Only there till seven. I have the evening shift tomorrow."

I nodded. I wasn't a fan of him working the night shift, only because of the journey home in the dead of night. "I can swing by before heading to Kirkby with Jacob and drive you in. It'll mean you're early though."

"That'd be great, thanks. I can perhaps go and grab a coffee or something first."

"I'll pick you up tonight too."

Lawrence's smile was sweet. "You know you don't

have to, right? I managed for months figuring out transport."

A tightening in my gut followed his words, reminding me what an asshole I'd been.

"Hey, I didn't say it for you to get that look on your face." He stroked his fingers over the creases between my brows, and I relaxed a little. "We've moved beyond all that, right?"

I hesitated, earning me a hard look that made my lips twitch. "Right. Still don't like how much of an asshole I was."

He snorted. "That you know you were an asshole is enough."

I searched his eyes, wondering if it really was.

This weekend had been a shitshow, which I'd expected it to be. And while we'd exchanged I love yous, which still hadn't fully registered yet, I couldn't forget his weird reaction to camping and dogs. To be honest, it had thrown me.

"What are you thinking?"

I didn't want to get into this now; instead, I focused on the one aspect of this weekend that still blew my mind. I wanted to absorb his words, feel them soul deep, wrap myself up in them, and finally register them fully. "I told you I loved you yesterday."

Delicious pink touched Lawrence's cheeks when I

spoke, peeking out from beyond his whiskers. His lips parted as he nodded. "Yeah. And I meant it when I told you I love you."

My morning wood twitched, liking the sound of that as much as my heart did. "Perhaps I need to show you as well." I angled my hips, brushing my groin against him. It had the effect I was after. Lawrence's breathing picked up, his gaze flicking to my mouth.

"How about you give me five minutes in the bathroom to get ready and then meet me in the shower?"

The twitch in my boxers took over, my dick pulsing and deciding it was an ass-seeking missile with how it was attempting to break through the thin fabric.

"I'll take that as a yes," Lawrence said with a chuckle, feeling my missile for himself.

I grinned. "That's a hell yes. My missile needs to find its mark."

Lawrence pulled back from the kiss he was going for, his eyes wide. "Missile?" His lips pursed together, his muscles tensing and shaking.

My grin stretched even wider. "You better believe it."

Laughter burst free from him, fast and loud and so perfect. "God, I love you." His words were garbled around his deep chortle. A fast kiss later, he left me breathless as I watched him disappear inside the joined bathroom. I grabbed hold of myself and winced, squeezing lightly.

Getting control of myself, I got my ass out of bed and went to the main bathroom in the house. After finishing up and managing a piss despite my painful cock, I brushed my teeth and headed back to my bedroom. When I entered, the bathroom door was ajar. I smiled, my junk perking up again when I stepped inside, my gaze immediately landing on Lawrence's wet back.

I stepped in beside him, belatedly casting a look to make sure he'd organized supplies. Seeing he had, I leaned into him, pressing against his crack, my chest to his warm skin. My lips found purchase. Angling his neck for me, he groaned when I kissed along the exposed flesh.

"Are you ready for me?" I asked, my voice husky.

"Why don't you check?"

My lips quirked as I continued to trace kisses over him before I reached for the lube. A moment later, I grabbed hold of myself when I discovered just how ready he was. "Fuck, you really are ready." My words and working fingers resulted in a long, low groan from him.

"Amazing what can be achieved," he mumbled,

breath catching as I caught the spot that I was sure had him seeing stars, "when you're given five minutes." He eased back against me, eager and so perfectly willing.

"You're so sexy like this." He seriously was. Already close to the tipping point, it wouldn't take much for either of us.

He turned his head, giving me access to his lips. I readily took his mouth with mine, loving the connection, the desperate cries combined with the clumsy kisses. When I pulled back, my gaze connected with his. Heavy-lidded, he was a picture of need.

As I sheathed myself, I willed myself to calm, to savor everything Lawrence was giving me. I pushed into him. With his face still angled so I could see at least part of his reaction, I watched as he closed his eyes, mouth parting.

"I love you," I said, inching in.

His lids sprung open, and I edged in further. And just as I bottomed out, he groaned around the words "Fuck, I love you too."

I didn't have time to smirk, to cry my satisfaction at his reaction. Instead, I moved. My plan for slow lovemaking went spiraling down the drain with the warm water. Moving fast, hips pistoning, legs shaking with every thrust, I groaned as he turned away, pressing his head against his arms on the tiled wall.

He matched every movement, each soft groan punctuated a moment later with a needy grunt. He slipped one hand down to take hold of his cock.

"Holy hell," he said with a gasp, his hand working.

The words pushed me over the edge. He tightened around me. The sensation was almost too much as I slammed my eyes closed.

I shuddered as I leaned against him, gasping for breath. Face against his back, I smiled, drawing my lids open. "You okay?"

"Urgh."

I laughed a little, regretting the movement immediately on my sensitive cock. "Is that a yes?"

"A hell yes," he said. Humor laced his words, the sound soothing.

"Brace yourself," I teased in warning as I held on to the latex and eased out of him.

He laughed in response, saying, "Did your missile survive?"

I snorted as I freed myself, tying off the condom before turning Lawrence around to face me. His grin was wide and contagious. "You better believe it. If we had more time, I'd show you just how powerful my weapon is."

He groaned and shook his head at me, pressing his

forehead against my chest. My laughter filled the room.

"Ready to eat?"

"Yeah, definitely," he said as he glanced up at me, the look in his eyes spreading new warmth through me.

This right here was just one version of what our love looked like. And I couldn't wait to discover every single aspect over time.

***

JACOB WAS ON FORM WHEN WE DROVE TO KIRKBY, making me laugh and entertaining Lawrence with stories of his youth. We'd dropped Lawrence off at Davis's coffee shop, armed with the skateboard that I begrudgingly thought he looked hot on, before heading onto the veterinary clinic.

"Molly," Carter said, smiling over at Jacob's dog and then shaking the man's hand once we'd made it over to him. "How you doing, Jacob?"

"Good, good. You?"

"Great, thanks." Carter turned his attention to me. "Hey, Billy, how are things in your world?" He shook my hand before indicating for us to follow him.

"Can't complain," I answered, more than aware I

wore a shit-eating grin still from my morning with Lawrence and the sweet kiss goodbye he gave me fifteen minutes ago.

Carter cocked his brow at me. "I can see that, but that smile you're wearing seems a lot more than a 'can't complain.'"

Jacob gave a deep snort, pulling both of our attention to the old man. "Just be grateful you get full sentences. He's been all starry-eyed since kissing that young man of his goodbye." He followed up with an eye roll. "Out on the street too. Not a care in the world who was watching." He shook his head, his eyes twinkling with humor. "Kids these days, no decorum. I would have been kicked in the ass if I'd kissed my Maggie May in the street like that."

"Ha. From the stories you've told me, I imagine you did a lot more in public than a small kiss."

Jacob cocked his brow at me. "Don't sass me, boy."

I laughed loudly. "Just one of many reasons why you're good for my ego, Jacob. 'Boy' and 'kid' in thirty seconds… you make me feel young."

"It seems like the rumors have substance," Carter said from his crouched position as he scratched Molly under her chin.

His gaze zeroed in on me. I met the look head-on. "I'm not even going to ask."

Carter smiled widely and shrugged, turning his attention to Jacob. "It wasn't Lawrence by any chance who Billy was behaving so inappropriately with, was it, Jacob?"

The twinkle remained in the old man's eyes. "My lips are sealed. But I'm sure if you head to the rainbow bar down the road, you'll hear all about it."

I laughed and shook my head. Ted and Jason did admittedly have a couple of rainbow pride stickers in the windows of their bar. Every time I saw them, I smiled, happy that there was a real sense of community in Kirkby and my own small hometown.

"I'll be sure to stop by a little later," Carter said, amused. He then focused on Molly. "And how's this young lady doing?"

Aware Jacob struggled to stand for long periods of time, I quietly headed toward the chair pushed against the wall while Jacob explained his concerns for Molly. When I placed the plastic chair down, I maneuvered him into the seat without fuss.

"I'll have a good look in her ears and see what's going on," Carter said after listening to Jacob explain how Molly had cried a couple of times when she'd had her ears rubbed, and she'd been shaking her head a lot. "Billy, you mind holding her head for me?"

"Sure thing." I got to my knees, wincing a little

when I fell a little too heavily on my old injury.

"You all right there?" Carter's voice held concern.

"Yeah, just feeling it this morning is all." Truth was, my knee had gone through a lot more strain over the past couple of months. From carrying Lawrence around to kneeling and bending a whole lot more when Lawrence and I screwed like bunnies, my knee had felt the pressure. And I had zero regrets, though should probably find a local physio or something to get some strengthening exercises.

"I bet," Carter said quietly, though not quiet enough to stop the words reaching Jacob, who gave a hearty chortle.

I simply shook my head, holding back my laugh and my blush as I focused on settling Molly so Carter could examine her.

After inspecting her ears, Carter stood and said, "Definitely an ear infection. A course of antibiotics should clear them up quickly."

I dotted a kiss on Molly's head and told her she was a good girl before I stood, this time schooling my reaction to my ache.

"I'll get her first few drops in and get the medicine labeled up for you, then you should be good to go."

"Thanks, Dr. Carter." Jacob reached out, and Carter shook his hand once he'd administered the eardrops.

"Anytime. Just be sure to let me know next Monday if she's still in any discomfort, okay?"

"Will do, Doc."

I shook Carter's hand while subtly watching Jacob as he stood, making sure he got up okay. Once he was on his two feet, I gave my full attention to Carter. "Thanks for that," I said.

"Absolutely." He studied me a moment, a small smile on his face. "So, now that you guys are official, perhaps we could arrange something." He paused. "You are official, right?" At my smirk and head bob, he continued, "That's great. Perhaps come by for dinner one night? Maybe next weekend or something?"

I liked the sound of that.

Since moving, beyond Austin and more recently, Jasper, I hadn't made an effort to put myself out there and make friends. When I'd been invited to Ted and Jason's get-together in July, the offer had taken me by surprise. So extending that group, especially as a couple with Lawrence, sounded good.

"Yeah, sounds good. Thanks. Let me chat with Lawrence"—his mouth twitched at the use of his name, which we'd previously avoided—"and check it's okay. He's working Friday night and Sunday till early evening, so Saturday's the best bet."

"Excellent. We'll provisionally plan for Saturday,

but let me know."

I smiled. "Sounds good." I turned and checked that Jacob was doing okay. He was smiling down at Molly, stroking her neck. "You ready, Jacob?"

"Sure am, if you two have finished setting up your dinner plans."

I snorted at him. "We have. Come on. I'll treat you to a tea and a slice of something good before we head back if you want."

Jacob grinned at that. "I wouldn't say no to one of those caramel eclairs if they've got any left."

We said goodbye to Carter, headed out to reception, where Jacob settled the bill, and made our way to the coffee shop. I didn't even attempt to hold back my smile when I saw Lawrence sitting at an outside table, Davis standing next to him. A quick glance at the time told me he had another ten minutes before he had to be at work.

"Hey," I greeted, interrupting them. I pulled out one of the empty chairs for Jacob, who took it with a grunt and a "Thanks." I then immediately leaned in and placed a solid kiss on Lawrence's mouth. His cheeks pinkened, the sight making wings take flight in my stomach.

I didn't think I'd ever tire of that reaction from him, or my own to the sweetness he gave me.

I looked up at Davis, ready to greet him, and was met with a huge grin and raised brows.

"Well, this explains so much," Davis said, reaching out to shake my hand. His focus moved to Jacob, and he reached out to say hello. Once his attention turned back to me, Davis said, "So the trip away was a success then?"

I kept my smile fixed, not wanting to share anything Lawrence didn't want to. "Well, this happened a few weeks before this weekend away," I offered, deflecting attention away from Lawrence's sister's wedding and back on us.

"Huh." Davis cast his eyes on Lawrence. "I'm impressed you kept that quiet."

Lawrence rolled his eyes. "The gossip mill's been going. I'm more than aware of that."

"True." Davis nodded. "It's a good development. We'll have to get together for dinner sometime."

I laughed, and Jacob quickly joined in.

"You'll have to get in line," Jacob said, still chortling. "Anyone would think it was the second coming or something with the news of these two courting." He shook his head. "Careful, Billy, they'll be organizing a parade or something in your honor at this rate. A special one celebrating coupledom."

I rolled my eyes at the old man. "Don't be saying

that in public, for Christ's sake. You'll give someone ideas."

Lawrence's groan drew my attention to him. Wide-eyed, he shook his head. "Seriously, don't. If Ted gets wind of even the word parade, one will definitely be happening."

"Well," Davis said, his voice taking on a tone that had me narrowing my eyes, "I know for a fact that Ted has very loudly suggested a pride parade of sorts. Jason's been keeping him reined in"—he shrugged —"but I think it's quite a cool idea. A small pride parade for the four local towns."

"If you've still got one of those caramel eclairs I like, Davis, I'll gladly wave any flag you want me to and put in a good word with Mrs. Higgins, who's the head of that women's institute group. You need support? She's the woman who makes things happen."

My brows lifted high. "Jacob O'Connor," I said with a laugh, "you sly dog. You been holding out on me?"

He looked up at me, quirking one of his bushy white brows. "You're not the only one who knows how to woo someone pretty and a few years younger."

Lawrence choked on his water, Davis laughed loudly, and I gaped at him. I closed my mouth and looked at Lawrence, who was mopping up his spillage with a napkin. With a smile, I said, "Well, there's no denying you're pretty."

Lawrence shook his head at me and flipped me off. "And that's my cue to bounce," he said, saying goodbye to a laughing Davis and Jacob and pressing his mouth to mine before mumbling, "I'll show you just how pretty I can be later when you're swallowing my cock."

Wide-eyed and I was sure red-faced, I all but swallowed my tongue as I watched him saunter away, skateboard now on the ground, and him riding the shit out of the wooden board I was still convinced was a deathtrap.

"And I'm not even going to ask," Davis said, drawing my attention to him.

I shook my head, bemused and turned on. Lawrence certainly knew how to leave in style. Asshole. "Yeah, best not. Right, Jacob, tea and eclair, right?"

He nodded. "Sure is."

I grinned after him, then followed Davis inside to make our order.

There was no doubt having Lawrence in my life made life a damn sight better and me a whole bunch happier. And I was more than happy for the show-and-tell of every single pretty inch of the man I'd given my heart to.

CHAPTER EIGHTEEN

BILLY HAD MOMENTS OF BEING A FOOL. AND HIM HIDING how much he'd been struggling with his leg and knee over the past few weeks was just one instance. I rolled my eyes at him. "You're a dick for keeping this to yourself."

Despite his careless shrug, he at least had the good sense to look a little sheepish. "It's fine."

"Do I really need to remind you of some of the overprotective crap you said to me when I was healing?" I'd considered keeping my mouth shut. Billy was a grown-ass man, but his groans getting up out of bed weren't of the hot and heavy variety, and the winces were coming more often.

Thinking back, I was sure it had been happening before we headed to my sister's wedding, but only since being back had I started to pay attention. With the heaviness of seeing my mom no longer hanging over me, I was finally able to think beyond my anxiety.

And now, weeks later, he'd literally just admitted how much his old injury was hurting him, and the gentle jogs we'd been taking the past couple of weeks together no doubt had made it worse. I couldn't help but feel guilty that I'd egged him on to join me.

"You hated seeing me in pain, right?"

Billy raised his eyes to the ceiling. "I hear you. You've made your point." There was no bite to his tone.

I narrowed my eyes at him. "You're pissing me off even more that you're making me fret and shit at you." I glared at him. "I'm serious, loving you should have come with a warning label of some sort. I don't think I ever signed up for this role."

He grinned as his hands darted out to grab me. Taking hold of me, he tugged me closer, burying his head against my neck. "It's kind of sweet."

I snorted and jabbed my fingers into his side. "Hardly. I'm sounding as bad as you did when you kept going off at me, and that was before you professed your undying love for me." I laughed loudly when he tackled me to the sofa. I landed with an oomph, his heavy form making me groan, both from the weight and the welcome contact.

When he angled up, what I called his dopey, loved-up grin was on his face. It came out every so often. It was one of my favorites on him. "I promise to find someone local for therapy, okay? Get some strengthening exercises and whatever."

"Good." I leaned up and brushed my lips against his mouth. When I pulled away, I scowled up at him. "Do not even think about it unless you can back it up." He was hard against my groin, and my cock perked up with a happy twitch.

He sighed and once more buried his face against my neck.

"You could just blow me," I said. I grinned widely when he rose up and peered down at me. "If you go on a mission and use that tongue of yours, I bet we'd have enough time."

"You're killing me, baby."

And that ridiculous endearment hit me right in the chest. Every damn time. "Screw it. Let me suck you off instead," I said, bucking up against him. The asshat knew exactly what he was doing, not only with his words, but when he moved his hand and placed his pointer finger on my lip, tapping.

I opened immediately and sucked hard, loving the

flare of his eyes, the way his pupils blew. And when his mouth parted, I all but tore at his clothes to get to him.

"Shit." He tugged away from me, taking me by surprise. "They're here." Jerking, he jolted up, knee brushing my cock, making me grunt and shift back quickly. "Fuck, you okay?" he said, eyes wide and laughter in his voice.

"Urgh." My snort followed. "My balls will survive another day."

Billy beamed down at me, his eyes bright. "Come on. Georgia will only give me shit if I keep her waiting." He dotted a kiss to my lips and then stood, taking my hand and helping me up.

"That's not helping the situation in my pants," I grumbled, following behind Billy to the door and readjusting myself. Billy glanced back at me, pulling out the flannel shirt he had tucked into his pants.

"We'll have to survive." He chuckled and opened the front door just as the engine of the white Hyundai cut off.

I hung back as Billy stepped forward, giving him the opportunity to greet Georgia. It had been a long time since they'd seen each other, and their relationship had been strained at the time. Things had changed since then. Between Billy's PTSD support and both Billy and Georgia moving states to start afresh had resulted in regular calls and now this first visit.

And this time with Russell, her boyfriend in tow.

After the last nightmare meeting of family, this one already felt like a walk in the park. I was excited to meet the woman who knew Billy from another time, was looking forward to hearing stories. There was still Billy's large blood family to meet, which was the plan over the New Year, but this was just as significant.

"You're a sight for sore eyes, Hilton." The dark-haired woman wrapped him in a fierce hug. She barely reached his shoulders, but from Billy's grunt, I expected she had a strong hold. Before he could respond beyond hugging her back, my attention moved to the two boys who stepped out of the vehicle, shoving at each other.

Jaylen was a head taller than Alex—their difference in sizes making it easy for me to identify who was who. Both had shaggy brown hair and the gangly limbs of growing boys. Jaylen stretched, pushing his hair out of his eyes, then looking around, his gaze landing on me. An awkward chin lift was sent my way, bringing a smile to my face. At fourteen, he was already taller than his mom, and almost as tall as the man who stepped away from the driver door.

After a quick glance at Georgia and a small smile,

he made eye contact with me. I stepped forward immediately, stretching out to take his hand.

"Hey, Russell. Lawrence. Good to meet you."

His firm grip clasped mine before he released, his smile already on his face. He was a good-looking guy with friendly, bright blue eyes and a healthy collection of laughter lines. "You too."

"Journey okay?" I asked.

"Not too bad. The flight was on time, and we picked up the rental okay." He angled over to look at Georgia and Billy when their soft conversation cut off, and Billy shouted at the boys to get their butts over to him.

"I'll be," Billy said, pulling both boys into a hug, ignoring their scrunched noses and stiff limbs. "What the heck are you feeding these boys, Georgia?" He pressed a kiss to each boy's head, and while they weren't gushing in response, they weren't fighting it either. Alex gave up quicker than his big brother and put his arm around Billy. Not long after, Jaylen followed suit. The sight sent a shot of warmth through me.

"And you are far too young and handsome to be Lawrence." Georgia was before me, a wide smile spread across her mouth as she took me in. "Already I can tell you're too good for him," she jested with a wink before wrapping me up in her arms.

She really did have a tight grip. Motherly. Similar to the ones I'd received from Grace growing up. I snorted inwardly at the thought that I received more comfort from the housekeeper than my own mom.

I hugged her back, pulling away with a laugh, saying, "I think we're just about right for each other."

My words lit up her eyes, her brows lifting as she studied me more carefully. With a tilt of her head, she said, "You know what, I think you may be right."

Lightness settled in my chest. While there'd been no real nerves about meeting Georgia, the connection to Billy and his past was important. As such, perhaps I'd been more on edge than I realized. "Come on. Let's get in and make coffee. The boys can help me sort the bags later," I said and led them into Billy's house.

Once inside, everyone washed up quickly and finally exhaled when they sat.

"I know it's not that long a flight, but with travel times to and from the airport, it makes it a big day," Georgia said, hand resting easily on Russell's leg.

Billy eyed her hand before pulling his gaze away. While he'd warned me that he felt odd about meeting Russell, I was still surprised by his obvious discomfort.

"The plane stink doesn't help," I said once it was

clear Billy was caught up with his thoughts and wouldn't answer. "It warps time even more."

Georgia snorted. "Plane stink is about right." She shuddered. "There's a whole bunch of weirdos out there. The quirky, awesome kind—those I welcome gladly. It's the others wearing socks with sandals and those who cough into their hands, then touch everything that pushes me close to the edge."

Russell laughed. "Close? That implies you've not reached tipping point and can walk away."

She nudged him, saying, "Hey! Of course I was going to call that woman out. Sneezing and then touching the door and the screens…." She shuddered. "I just can't."

"I admit there are some individuals who make empathy a little difficult." Russell's lips twitched when he spoke.

"What Russell means is some people are dickheads. He's just too polite to say." Georgia squeezed his leg, and I side-eyed Billy, who was beginning to freak me out a little with how quiet he was being.

"How about I show the boys and Russell where you're all going to be sleeping the next few nights," I said, needing to cut this tension. There was no doubt Georgia would use the opportunity to call Billy out on his silence. I hoped them having the opportunity to talk this out was the right thing.

Georgia's gaze met mine, and she gave me a small smile before flicking her focus to Billy, who stood and started collecting the empty coffee mugs.

"Righto. Jaylen, Alex, let's go get settled," Russell said to the boys. Their head bobs and smiles were immediate. And I was impressed as hell that they placed down their phones without fuss and stood, heading to the front door. Russell followed after and sent a cursory glance to Billy, who'd headed to the kitchen. There were no telltale signs of him loading the dishwasher or rinsing the mugs.

I hesitated.

"I'll talk to him." Georgia's hand on my forearm made me jump.

I chuckled despite my concern. "Jesus, I didn't see you there. Some impressive ninja skills you've got going on."

She laughed lightly. "Years of tiptoeing around kids to first not wake them, and now to catch them up to no good." She winked, her smile losing some of its shine. "He'll be fine. He may just need some sense knocked into him."

I nodded, sure a conversation would at least settle some of whatever was going through Billy's mind.

Before I left, I said quietly, "Just go easy on him. He's been struggling recently, physically, and needs to get some physio support." I offered a shrug, hoping she read between the lines that his discomfort could easily have awoken pain of the crash.

Georgia smiled sadly. "I will."

I bobbed my head in thanks and headed outside, pulling the door behind me before going on to show Russell the apartment for him and Georgia. Not wanting to head back to the main house to show the boys where they'd be sleeping, I pulled out my skateboard after Jaylen had spotted it.

Alex studied me once we were outside on the concrete drive. "You're a grown-up, but you skateboard?"

I laughed. "Well, yeah. I'll clue you into something though, Alex. I regularly don't feel like a grown-up."

Russell laughed and nodded in agreement. "It's true. It's only when I look in a damning mirror or try and touch my toes first thing in the morning that I'm reminded I'm fifty-two rather than twenty-one."

"That's just weird," Alex said with the truth of an eleven-year-old. "How can you not feel like an adult when you're both so old?"

My snorting laughter ripped out of me at that.

"Thanks, dude. I'm not that old. Well, I didn't feel like I was until this conversation."

Alex simply shrugged with a grin. "Go on then. Show us what you can do."

I could tell by both his and Jaylen's faces that they expected me to fall flat on my face, and I hoped to hell I wouldn't. Suffering that humiliation in front of these kids was a hard no. I was only partly joking to myself. My skateboard, or versions of it, had been something I'd been attached to since Alex's age. While Mom had vehemently disapproved, with me rarely having anything even close to a social life growing up, she'd reluctantly given me the okay to skate on our tennis court.

I'd challenged myself, set myself tasks, new tricks to master and rule. And that hadn't changed over the years. While parkour had been my fixation for a good eight years, a skateboard had the added bonus of transport.

Since healing from my most recent injuries, I'd been back on my board, doing a few tricks that, while impressed, Billy found it difficult to watch, which I found hilarious.

And while I wouldn't push it and show off too badly in front of the boys, my ankle still not quite up to strength, my plan to impress them remained.

I rolled and turned a few times to get my rhythm. I did a couple of ollies first up, keeping it old school. Having caught their attention, I rolled into an alpha flip. Not the first I'd tried in the last few weeks, thank Christ, since I'd landed on my ass a couple of times.

I jumped, flicked, spun a hundred and eighty degrees, eyes on the board as it flipped beneath my feet. My feet found purchase as I continued to roll, a shit-eating grin on my face.

The round of applause from all three spectators greeted me when I stopped.

"That was incredible. Can you teach me that?" Alex said, excitement pitching his voice high.

I grinned and then looked at Russell, both of us a little wide-eyed at the request. "Maybe not that one. It took me a lot of falls and practice to get that one right."

Alex looked crestfallen, while Jaylen's shoulders slumped.

"Maybe once Lawrence has seen what you guys can do on a skateboard first, he could then teach you that first one. The ollie, did you call it?" Russell glanced at me, seeking approval.

I grinned. "Absolutely. I even have a spare board and some pads you can use. Perhaps mess around first, warm up, find your balance, then we can start?" I offered.

"Yes!" Alex fist-pumped, while Jaylen nodded, giving an I'm-too-cool-to-show-you-I'm-excited shrug.

"Awesome. Let me get you guys kitted out, then perhaps Russell and I can grab another coffee, but we can sit out here on the porch to watch how you're doin'. Sound good?" While that would mean heading back inside, we'd been gone for almost forty-five minutes, hopefully enough time for some sort of conversation to have taken place. And with Russell and me watching the boys, Billy and Georgia could either join us or carry on catching up. The choice was theirs.

It didn't mean I was eager to interrupt them though.

THE REST OF THE EVENING WASN'T PAINFUL EXACTLY, but Billy's silence was both pissing me off and concerning me and making Russell uncomfortable. And the latter annoyed the hell out of me too.

Russell was a good guy. Amazing, in fact. His love for both Georgia and the boys was obvious, which already was enough to make me like the man. But knowing what he did for a living? Hell, my respect jumped tenfold. What I would have done to have a guy like him on my side growing up.

An advocate of LGBTQ+ kids? I shook my head, struggling to put to words my admiration for him or the stories he shared.

The boys were in bed in the spare room, and we were out in the backyard on the veranda. Russell and I were drinking beer, Georgia wine, while Billy was on scotch, which I'd never known him to do other than on the anniversary of Clark's death.

Russell listened intently as I shared a little of my history with him. The beer made my tongue loose, but my sharing was more to do with me finally being in a safe space and no longer feeling like a transient.

With that in mind, I reached out and placed my hand on Billy's knee, startling him. His gaze turned to mine, his eyes letting me know he'd been in his own world and hurting.

"And this guy, right here," I said. My words were directed at Russell while my gaze fixed on Billy, "if you'd seen him being all commanding and Spartacus and shit...." I trailed off into a grin, my head a little woozy, but my heart happy.

My words broke through Billy's previous silence.

His brows quirked high, the right side of his mouth tilting up into a smile. "Spartacus?" The sadness from his eyes flipped into amusement and possibly bemusement from the two frown lines between his brows.

I shrugged. "Or you know, one of those *300* guys. That's Spartacus or something, right?"

This time he snorted, Russell and Georgia's laughter joining in.

"Or something," he said with a wink. "But you know it was a wedding, and I was in a suit, right?"

Some of the tension eased in me. He'd been listening to the discussion around him and not been as drawn inward as I'd feared. I bobbed my head, leaning into him a little more, playing up my drunken state and taking advantage of it completely. "You looked hot in that too." I dotted a kiss on his mouth, pulled back, and returned my attention to our guests who sat opposite us, snuggled together on the couch. Both looked entertained by my declaration. I was more than okay with that.

"And then, it just fell into place perfectly when the chief of police of all people, and this cute guy—" I jerked my head immediately in Billy's direction and smiled as I said, "—who I was definitely not interested in—" He snorted as I turned back to Georgia and Russell. "Anyway, this cute guy who doesn't hold a candle to my hot boyfriend, Billy here, who also happens to be both gay and well connected, they walked into at least the latter part of Billy's hero speech where he put the governor in her place." I took a large gulp of beer and sighed contently, even happier when I thought back to the brief conversation I'd had with Cody when he'd called us up a couple of weeks back. "Best roast ever."

"You managed to say your piece by yourself all the same." There was a sweet softness to Billy's voice that had me focusing on him. A gentle smile touched his lips. "If anyone was the Spartacus in this situation, it was you."

My mouth stretched wide. "Even if I have no clue who Spartacus is. He was a cool guy, right?"

Billy and Russell both laughed at that, Russell saying, "Yeah, he was the coolest for sure."

When Russell spoke, Billy looked directly at the man, his smile for the first time not dropping. "There was something about Kirk Douglas in that role."

Russell nodded. "Exactly. It didn't take Greg much to convince me when we were kids that he filled out his gladiator kit perfectly."

I took Billy's hand in mine, relaxing even more at Billy finally behaving like the man I knew him to be.

"Greg's your brother, right?" Billy asked.

At the question, I cast a quick glance at Georgia. She visibly sighed, sinking further, finally relaxing into the couch. I understood her reaction completely.

"Yeah. He's the reason why I do what I do. For work," Russell clarified. Georgia reached out and took his hand when he spoke, and my brows dipped, wondering if that was a show of support or simply enjoying the contact. "He was sixteen when he committed suicide."

"Fuck." The word slipped out, and I cringed, quickly saying, "Shit, sorry, man. That's... I don't know. I have no words, other than I can't imagine how difficult that must be for you."

Russell's smile was soft and seemed genuine. "Thanks. It was obviously a long time ago now, but he was my kid brother. I was away at college. I'd known he was gay. I'd been the only one he'd opened up to." He shrugged before lightly sighing. "Until someone else found out and made his life hell. That got worse when my parents found out and sent him to conversion therapy."

I placed down my bottle and squeezed Billy's hand, feeling sick to my stomach.

"He took his life four weeks in."

"Russell changed his degree and has made it his life

work supporting LGBTQ+ youth," Georgia said, pride evident in every syllable.

Russell responded with a small grin that screamed of his embarrassment. "Georgia forgets that I'm not a one-man band. I don't wear a cape or anything."

"Not all superheroes wear capes," Billy and Georgia said at the same time, their eyes connecting immediately, something silent passing between them.

A huff of laugh spilled out of Billy, drawing my attention to him.

"What?" I asked.

The smile on his face was gentle. "That's what Clark always used to say."

"Practically every damn day," Georgia added, her own smile sitting wistfully on her lips.

"Jesus, I haven't thought about that for years," Billy said, shaking his head.

I stroked my thumb over his hand, liking that his smile hadn't slipped.

"Do you know, Alex does the same high-pitched snort laugh that Clark did?" Georgia glanced over at Russell, who offered her a small wink.

"He does?" Billy asked. "Poor kid." He followed up with a chortle. "As long as both of the boys are better at telling jokes and don't go around scratching their balls in public like their dad did, I think they'll be okay."

I smiled when he continued to laugh and share stories about Clark. And when Georgia pulled Russell into the conversation a time or two, and no fireworks exploded, and the conversation didn't come to a screeching halt, my relief eased into my cells, making my eyes droop.

I hadn't had a fresh beer for a while, sobering me up a little more and making me ready for bed. It was Billy nudging me and me looking at him bleary-eyed that made me realize I'd been spending a fair amount of time dozing off.

"Come on, baby. Bedtime."

My smile was immediate as I held on to his hand, letting him haul my ass off the couch. Looking around, I realized that Russell and Georgia were already up and putting on their shoes. "Sorry, kinda dozed off there," I said sheepishly, wondering how the youngest of the bunch was such a lightweight.

"No problem. It's way past our bedtime. Fair warning, Jaylen sleeps in, and we usually have to drag him out of bed, but Alex tends to wake up at ridiculous o'clock." Georgia grinned, saying, "And we'll happily have a lie in tomorrow."

Billy grunted. "Is she still a slacker, Russell?"

Russell shook his head. "I wouldn't dare answer either way." He took her hand in his. "Come on, bed." He then looked back at us, saying, "You sure you don't need us early to help with preparation or anything?"

"We're all good and prepared. Even had an extra call to Mom this morning to check up on a few things," Billy answered. It was sweet that he'd made that call, asking questions about the turkey for tomorrow's Thanksgiving meal. His mom sounded great and had already managed to corner me on a couple of calls, letting me know how excited she was for our visit over the New Year. With how welcoming she was, it was easy to be excited rather than nervous.

"Great. Good night then. Good luck with the boys," Russell said, waving a hand over his shoulder as he and Georgia left.

We said goodbye and locked up, Billy doing another sweet thing by sticking his head around the door of the boys' room to check up on them. Reassured they were fine, he stepped out, closing the door behind him while I stood grinning sleepily at him.

"What?" he asked as we headed to his room that was unofficially our room. "What's that smile for?"

I shrugged, not wanting to get heavy tonight after the tension of the day. "Just happy your family are here." While they were technically friends, I knew their connection went deeper than that. "And I'm proud of you," I said, unable to stop myself from dipping even a little into Billy's reaction today.

When his brows lowered in confusion, he asked, "Any reason?"

I licked my bottom lip before saying, "I know today took you by surprise." That was putting it mildly for sure, but he'd understand what I was getting at. "Yet you managed to work yourself to the point where your smile was genuine and talked about Clark and laughed while sharing stories. So, I'm proud of you." I gave a one-shoulder shrug.

As he tugged off his T-shirt in silence, he sat on the bed, throwing the shirt on the floor. "Bit me in the ass," he eventually said, making me snort. I sat down close and pressed my thigh against his. "I thought I'd got my head around losing Clark, Georgia moving on, you know? She deserves to be happy, more than anyone I know, but being here, for that split second, I expected to see Clark step out of the car, which makes no sense at all. It's been years." He stopped talking, and I moved my hand to his.

"It's okay that things don't make sense. And it's okay to be sad and angry, but not at Georgia or Russell. And I know you know that, and that's why I'm proud of you."

Turning his face toward me, he smiled. "Get your ass over here." A tug and a shift later, I straddled him on the bed, both still sitting on the edge. "You've carried me today."

"It was my turn, right? We share the load, share it all."

"You know, I could say something about giving you my load—"

I shoved him back, cutting him off, both of us laughing. "That was weak, dude, even for you."

"Okay, *dude*," he emphasized, "but yeah, you're right. That you're in my corner is pretty damn great. Thank you."

I stared down at him, nodding. "It is, and it's not you who needs to be thanking me."

"It's not?"

"Nope. We're in this together, right?"

Billy nodded in answer.

"So we show each other every day how thankful and happy we are. I know you appreciate me—"

"And I know you do me as well," he said, cutting me off, reaching up and stroking against my facial hair that I really needed to trim.

"So the only thing we need to do is keep being open and cutting through the bullshit." I searched his eyes, watching him drink in every word. Never in my life having had a conversation like this before, it was as nerve-wracking as it was effortless. A strange combination. "And after we get back in the new year, perhaps it's finally time we start thinking about those dogs."

Yanking me down, he smiled widely at me. "That sounds very doable."

"Yeah?" I asked.

"Definitely," he agreed. He sealed his response with a kiss that had me losing my breath and hauling him into the en suite bathroom, knowing how creaky our mattress was and not wanting to have any awkward conversations tomorrow.

And as Billy woke me up in every way imaginable in the shower, I knew without a doubt that what we had would stick. Despite misunderstandings, overreactions, and sometimes confusion, all that had happened between us was as it should be. And my old friend karma was welcome any damn time she wanted when she brought me a man who understood me inside and out.

And here, right now, and in this moment, there was nowhere I would rather be.

IT WAS A FULL-ON DAY, AND ALL BECAUSE TED HAD gotten his way by creating a community pride festival in the area. The four local towns had combined, staging the festivities in Kirkby. There was a small parade, a collection of fun booths, some raising funds for a couple of LGBTQ+ charities, and some local-talent showcases.

I looked on, an equal mix of pride and anxiety as Lawrence launched into the air on his skateboard, the collection of onlookers applauding loudly, some gasping. I was definitely in the gasping group as my heart flipped over itself, threatening to leave my body with the force.

There wasn't a chance I'd ever talk him out of doing the crazy skateboard stunts that he loved, or even the parkour, but it didn't mean I could witness his adrenaline-junkie stunts without being close to puking.

"How are you doing over here?" Cody's question pulled my gaze in his direction.

I smiled, taking the leash from him and bending down and patting Pippa on the head. Our collie, which Lawrence and I had rescued from a local shelter about six months ago, wagged her tail happily before jumping up, her paws landing on my thighs, demanding more fuss. "Other than being close to having a heart attack every time his board leaves the ground, I'm good," I answered. "Did Pippa behave herself?"

"She did. Even managed to get me a phone number from a cute guy over at the small petting zoo." He waggled his brows, making me snort.

I shot Cody a grin. "Nice. You planning on using it?"

He shrugged. "Maybe. I'm in town for a couple more days so I'm not completely against a casual hookup. The guy was cute."

I nodded at that, wondering what type of man he was into. I thought back to when we'd first met at Lawrence's sister's wedding and how he'd seemed keen on Lawrence. It was impressive really that we'd all kept in touch, considering that shitshow of a visit.

I supposed that's what battling dragons did. It brought you closer. It was just a relief we'd done so successfully. Cody had called us during the last election, letting us know with unreserved glee that Governor Crawford had lost. After leaving Wisconsin, I'd hoped karma would step in again and give Melissa her comeuppance. She hadn't disappointed.

"I know you'd prepared me for my visit," Cody then said, "but I hadn't realized there was such a strong community here. How's that even possible?" Genuine awe lit his words, and I understood his reaction.

"Just lucky I guess. It's amazing what a few strong personalities can do in a town like this. Best decision I ever made was moving away from Chicago. Honestly, I couldn't imagine being anywhere else."

"I can definitely see the appeal," Cody said, focus moving back to Lawrence, his eyes widening.

My heart stuttered at his reaction, my ears also tuning in to the noise around me. A gasp. A caught breath. In the split second that it took me to turn and look at what caused the reaction, my heart plummeted.

With growing dread, I turned to look, hoping with

everything in me that Lawrence was okay, that he wasn't injured. Considering I was expecting the worst—Lawrence not making his big finale flip, which I'd watched him practice countless times—I was not expecting this.

Wide-eyed, I looked ahead. I forgot to breathe. Failed to get my brain firing correctly.

Lawrence was in the middle of the skate ramp, on one knee, an open box in his hand.

Holy shit. He was proposing and I'd missed it.

In my stupor, Pippa took off, easily freeing herself from my loose grip. She launched at Lawrence, tackling him with enthusiastic licks. The crowd laughed, but I didn't glance around, my eyes still firmly on the man who was my everything.

His grin stretched wide as he held onto Pippa's leash, moving her to his side. "Pippa seems to think your answer's going to be yes." He repositioned the box, this time removing the ring. And still I remained frozen, completely taken by surprise by the turn of events.

"I think that's your cue," Cody whispered close to my ear, his hand moving to my back. He didn't push, but it was enough of a wake-up for me to nod and react.

As I took the few steps to get to the ramp, my heart

somersaulted, emotions rising quickly and clogging my throat. By the time I reached Lawrence, I was already nodding, my grin stretched wide.

"Is that a yes, you will marry me?"

I swallowed hard, wanting to control myself enough to get my words out. "Yes," I said with a small laugh. "I'd love to." I reached down and took his free hand, tugging him to stand.

In the next breath, a ring was on my finger, feeling strange but so damn right, and my lips were fused with his. I was mildly aware of a happy bark and continued clapping and a few hollers, but my attention was all Lawrence's.

Between mistakes and healing, and forgiveness and courage, I'd never been happier than to have reached the point where I had officially *un*dicked myself. There wasn't a chance I'd ever take this man or this life we'd built for granted again.

BE ON THE LOOK OUT FOR MORE IN THIS SERIES, ALL IN the form of novellas. A gorgeous nurse will be getting his own book very soon. Be sure to be signed up to receive my **newsletter** so you don't miss out.

If you're look for more sweet heat, be sure to check

out *NOT USED TO CUTE*, my lovely Aussie stand-alone romance. **A bar owner who's not looking for a relationship. A lost soul who's afraid to trust. When Elijah and Seb meet, sparks fly. But will either of them find the courage to take what they want?**

If you're looking for sharp wit and something a little grittier from me, you'll definitely want to check out *THICKER THAN WATER*. *Thicker Than Water* **is a MM urban fantasy romance featuring a smart-mouthed wolf shifter, who kicks arse and forgets to take names—because life's too short for that admin shit!**

ACKNOWLEDGMENTS

The village was strong with this one.

Every email, every message, every review helps to push away the doubt. Thank you for being part of my village.

Every edit, every design, every share means I'm not alone. Thank you for being part of my village.

Every hug, kiss, and shared laugh fills me with gratitude and love. Thank you for being part of my village.

It's so easy to lose faith and focus, listen to self-doubt, but my village keeps me strong and on track. And I adore each and every one of you.

ALSO BY BECCA SEYMOUR

Coming Home Collection

Realigned

Amalgamated

True-Blue Series

Let Me Show You (#1)

I've Got You (#2)

Becoming Us (#3)

Thinking It Over (#4)

Always For You (#4.5 TED & JASON'S STORY - FREE for newsletter subscribers)

It's Not You (#5)

Urban Fantasy Romance

Thicker Than Water

Stand-Alone Contemporary

Not Used To Cute

ABOUT THE AUTHOR

I live and breathe all things book related. Usually with at least three books being read and two WiPs being written at the same time, life is merrily hectic. I tend to do nothing by halves, so I happily seek the craziness and busyness life offers.

Living on my small property in Queensland with my human family as well as my animal family of cows, chooks, and dogs, I really do appreciate the beauty of the world around me and am a believer that love truly is love.

To check for updates head to my website:
https://beccaseymour.com
You can sign up for my newsletter here:
https://landing.mailerlite.com/webforms/
landing/r9f0i4
Plus, join my Facebook group, which I share with the
awesome Louisa Masters here:
https://www.facebook.com/
groups/seymourbookswithmasterfulmen/

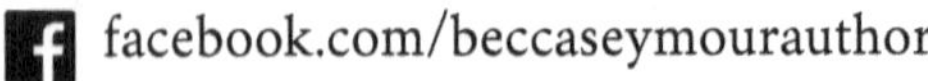

facebook.com/beccaseymourauthor
twitter.com/beccaseymour_
instagram.com/authorbeccaseymour
bookbub.com/authors/becca-seymour

www.ingramcontent.com/pod-product-compliance
Lightning Source LLC
Chambersburg PA
CBHW060903190726
48286CB00002B/350